Soul Family Six: The Chosen Series

ISBN: 978-1-963239-61-4

Published by **American Book Publisher**

For Inquiry

info@americanbookpublisher.com

www.americanbookpublisher.com

Table of Contents

SERIES ONE
SOUL FAMILY SIX
The Gifted

SERIES ONE
SOUL FAMILY SIX
The Gifted

SUMMARY

Seven new soul classmates Ariel, Germain,Gabriel, Angela, Lucifer,Lilith, and Chloe were very gifted from creation, and formed a bond that goes on to showcase their gifts in the Sacred Land of Harts until two violated the code of the Land, Lucifer and Lilith to force two of their classmates, Germain and Ariel, along with Archangel Michael, to take them down in an attack that caused a Revenge of a lifetime between Germain, Ariel, Lucifer, and Lilith.

Chapter 1
First Day of Sacred Pre- School

My name is Ariel, a new soul created in the Land of Sacred Hart. I'm new to the land and curious about what it means to be here and what it all has to offer. My guardian is Jophiel. She will help me understand what my duties are as a new soul and give me the guidance and help I need to understand my assignments.

I am four years old, and of course I am at the age where I will have to go to pre-school to prepare me for grade school. I am so excited because I feel like I can meet more souls my age to connect and learn from them. There were a total of 6 souls my age in my pre-school class.

The first two souls I met were Lucifer and his sister Lilith. They appeared to be very smart and had a knowing of things that seemed all so new to me. They were an interesting pair that I wanted to know more about.

The next two souls I met from my class were Gabriel and Angela. They were very quiet souls, but very friendly. I wanted to get to know them too, yet they were so very different from the last two I met.

The third set of souls I met were Germain and Chloe. It's safe to say I liked all my classmates, but the one that stood out the most to me was Germain. I couldn't stop smiling when we talked, but I enjoyed talking to him and was always excited to see him and I believe the same could be said for him.

Saint Michael was our pre-school instructor and he tested us daily on different things our souls desired and how we would apply that later to assignments in the land once old enough to perform them. Germain and I both replied, we are old enough now to perform. We have desires. We then laughed because we shared the same sentiment and replied at the same time. Saint Michael laughed as well, and replied, you two are most definitely spirit's kids. You have the heart of one.

As we were leaving class, there was a loud blast out in the schoolyard. Saint Michael escorted us to the safety shelter for souls our age, but Germain and I hid under Saint Michael's coat to see what was happening because he ran out to check. There were dark forces that I had never laid eyes on that were destroying the schoolyard. Saint Michael discovered us and first fussed at us for following him out, and then he gave us protective gear to protect ourselves against all dark forces. We stood up to them and fought with the rest of the angels. We weren't quite angels yet; we had to earn our wings, but we were on our way from that day forward. Saint Michael was really impressed with our bravery and called us the gifted ones, but he ordered us to be obedient if something like that ever happens again, and our reply was, yes, sir.

Chapter 2
Grade School

We made it through preschool, and now we're on to grade school. Grade school was fun but a little more serious in how we developed our skills. Our instructor was Saint Haniel. She taught us all about our sensory skills and how to detect what was safe and unsafe in our environment by using all of our senses. We also learned creativity, which was outsourced through fairyland.

Our first lesson was in creativity, and we left the site to learn this in fairyland. It was a vast land, but everyone there was small, and it was beautiful, perfect for souls our age. Of course, I had the same classmates from preschool, so it felt like an experience I got to learn and enjoy with family. Our off-site instructor was Mr. Tinker. He tasked us with creating things in our minds and bringing them to life, both mentally and physically. I had the most difficult time with this, while all my other classmates excelled at it. I was starting to get discouraged because I knew that the biggest achievement in the Sacred Land of Harts was to earn your wings, and the higher you ranked, the bigger your wings and authority.

At this rate, I would only be a citizen there if I couldn't accomplish this. Germain saw how I struggled in class, so he worked with me after class to help me tap into my creativity. I was improving, so hope was restored. Something mysterious happened in Fairyland one day when Germain and I decided to work after class. An unknown dark force appeared, which had never happened before in Fairyland, attacking the village. Everyone was terrified and in shock because nothing of this level had ever reached this faraway land. Something dark was among us, but it had to be our own because this world only allowed purity in it.

Germain and I got creative in order to protect this land from any more destruction and chaos. We developed a skill that united our thoughts and actions into one to build something bigger. We had been practicing it but never used it, never realizing we ever would, but nevertheless, glad we did. We cast a spell, returning the dark force from whence it came, and built a field over the whole land to protect it from anything coming in or going out. Because of our bravery and teamwork and my mastery of creativity, we were named honorary members of Fairyland, which I absolutely loved and took great pride in. I was a young soul and had mastered something that seemed to be an obstacle to me; testing my abilities became something I was honored for. It couldn't get much better than that, and it restored my hope to get my wings.

Although I had mastered the skill of creativity, in the Sacred Land of Harts, I needed to master perception and intuition. Mastering these skills came a bit easier for me after using my creative abilities, and I'm glad we took those classes first. It meant everything to me to exceed my goals and finish grade school on top. The top 3 students, upon being promoted, would receive their very own unicorn, mystical creatures from Fairyland sent to help in our magical abilities before reaching middle school. They enhance our skills with animals and creatures, increasing our intuition. I wanted that so badly and worked extremely hard to achieve it.

As the end of the school year approached, I was excited to find out if I was one of the top 3 students to receive a Unicorn for my hard work and efforts and be at the top of my class. On this particular day, all my classmates and I decided to walk to school together to discuss who would get a unicorn upon completion. I noticed a flower that was withering; that never happens in the Sacred Land of Harts. Something wasn't right; I could feel it, so we all investigated it. I carry magic dust with me as I am an honorary member of Fairyland. I sprinkled it in the air and spoke, "Reveal to me the unseen, that I cannot see, that happened before we arrived." I saw a dark force sprinkle something harmful to plants and living things, using something from a bottle they kept on them to destroy all that is good. I cast a spell to remove the poison and bring life to what was withered.

Finally, we got to school, and all my classmates shared with Saint Haniel that she would have been proud to see me use the perceptions I learned in her class just on our way to school. She was excited to hear that, so she decided to do something she had never done for a class before. She awarded us all with a unicorn because we had worked together, and she knew we understood everything that was taught in her class. Somehow, I felt Haniel was responsible for what we saw in my vision on our way to school, and that some other light being close to our land was responsible for what happened in Fairyland, but I could not prove it. It just seemed as if my classmates and I were tested every time we neared completion of our courses. It may all be a test from Spirit. We may or may not ever know.

Chapter 3
Middle School

We are all a little bit taller, a little bit cuter, and a lot more excited about beginning school now to show off our knowledge and skills that we learned from previous years and the activities we did with our unicorns during school break.

I didn't get to spend much time with many of my classmates during our break from school, so I was excited to see them and start over again. I spent a lot of my time in advanced studies in Fairyland to learn alchemy, so I didn't get to do a lot of fun activities during our time out. It always seemed like more fun times were in school anyway.

The first soul being I came across on my path to school is Germain; he lived the closest to me, so we walked to school together. He told me what he planned to do and learn in the time we are in school and what he did in his downtime during the break from school. Seems we have a lot in common. We did the exact same thing, yet, I never ran into him during the time we were on our way to Fairyland or even while we were there. We were both driven and focused, that we didn't see each other or cross paths during the entire time of traveling there with our unicorns, and it may be partly because we transported there in a blink. Either way, it was really nice to see him.

We ran into Chloe, Gabriel, and Angela on the way to school too. They all talked about everything they learned over the break and how they were learning healing work, which is something I know we will all be learning next, and they have already experienced it. I was really excited to be in a class of souls that were equally ambitious as I was because they truly were my inspiration. We didn't see Lucifer or Lilith yet on the way in, but I know whatever they did during the break was as magnificent and that they were equally ambitious.

One of our instructors was a previous instructor we had that was promoted to an Archangel, which is really high level. Archangel Haniel is our instructor, and she will be working with us on healing with our hearts and minds, and our other instructor is Archangel Uriel. He will teach us how to guide others that will make us great leaders in our world and also the history of the land and really how to adapt if we ever have to face adversity.

I realized that the fun times we had in school prior to this day meant we really needed to focus. It might be fun, but not like before. We were maturing, and we would definitely be more mature after this school season was over. This was the school season when talk about the Wheel of Fortune was most common. We always passed it on our way to some of our off-site assignments but never grasped its meaning, other than it being beautiful and huge. It's said that upon completing high school, we would have to spin the Wheel of Fortune or Wheel of Destiny to decide our paths as older souls. Many souls didn't want their destiny predetermined; they wanted to choose their own path. I didn't quite have a viewpoint on it yet, but I knew I would at some point, so I released the thought.

This school season was very challenging and rewarding at the same time, and the time was coming up for review and the big exam. We hadn't had an exam in previous school seasons, but often felt as if we did because something always seemed to happen. This time, we were going to Sacred Heart Hospital to help with healing work on older souls and the recently injured during physical outside work for our exams in healing. After completion, we would be quizzed on the history of the land. I always felt like I needed to work harder than my other classmates to reach where they were already, and deep down, I felt like other souls knew it too. Everyone did well on their exam, but when my turn came to perform, there was something different about the soul I was trying to heal.

Their energy was dark, and I felt like it was trying to absorb mine. I immediately informed my instructor by astral projecting so she could intervene, as well as my classmates. It was a bitter fight, but we defeated it collectively as a class. I lost some of my strength from the absorption of my energy, but my instructor healed me. After waiting a while, I took the healing exam again to be graded fairly with my classmates, and I passed with flying colors, both in my history and healing exams. I was now ready to enter high school as a seasoned soul, along with all my classmates. I was excited for this new phase and couldn't wait to see what joy it would bring. During the break before high school began, my classmates and I decided to get ahead in our studies and practice our gifts together to grow stronger.

Chapter 4
High School

It's now the first day of Sacral Hart High School. The moment you walk in is intimidating. The school is huge and finding your way around is a chore in itself.

Luckily for my classmates and me, we knew our way around because we took the tour of the building before the school year began. Over the period of not having school, I would often come to the school and watch the choir perform. They sang so beautifully that I decided I wanted to be a part of it, and so did the rest of my classmates.

You could only be in extracurricular activities once you reached high school. It wasn't available to younger souls due to certain developments we needed to undergo first. We learned meditation, prayer, and devotion in high school. Younger souls get distracted easily, so of course, everything we are learning in high school held off until we were able to develop focus, as we will in meditation, which is similar to some things we have learned previously.

We studied meditation from Archangel Uriel, who taught at both the middle school and the high school. The best part of high school was being able to do extracurricular activities in between classes and after school. Lucifer loved being in the choir as much as I did. He was able to do solos and was even known for his wonderful angelic voice among the land. He was good at everything.

High school, to me, would have been a bit boring if other activities weren't available to us because we spent a lot of time in solitude, and singing brought out our creativity along with our playful side. We also had a performing arts program, and we often got a chance to bring life to what we wanted to draw, literally off the page. There were different forms of art, so you decided what you preferred.

I was starting to understand the chatter from middle school about doing something they wanted to do, but I also knew we were to be obedient to Spirit and trust his plan for each of us. I was conflicted in my energy, but I continued learning and enjoying what I've learned and also enjoying playtime to unwind a bit after a full day of meditation. I often felt more energized after we did it, and so did my classmates.

Chapter 5
Higher Learning Academy

Higher learning school was where many of us came to study everything related to our chosen fields. Mine was patience and law. It's where you delve into the fundamentals and deepen your understanding of your subject. My old classmates Gabriel and Angela taught this class. They were the most patient souls I had ever encountered and were perfect as my instructors. Archangel Michael taught the law classes. He headed the war department and also conducted training classes. I was excited about working with him again. When we first met, I was just a small soul, and now being taught by an instructor who has ascended to the rank of Archangel with his own division is truly inspiring.

It motivates me to apply what I learn here proudly every day. The classes taught by former classmates Gabriel and Angela were the most challenging for me. My thoughts often struggled to stay focused enough to manifest things with my mind. Since we were former classmates, they worked with me after class to help me develop patience in my thoughts and achieve greater precision. I was very grateful for their help, and by the time I finished at the school for higher learning, I had achieved patience.

Working with Archangel Michael was a completely different experience. There were so many moving parts both on the field and in the classroom. Unlike in childhood, where I had my classmates with me, this time it was just

Chloe and me. I would occasionally see her as we walked to classes or flew into school on our horses, but our assignments and learning paths were different. Chloe and I were the only ones in the class to receive a horse, but your horse chooses you; we don't choose it.

My horse was black, and most of the other horses in the land were white. So, being the only black one, she chose me, indicating that we were both one of a kind. I'm deeply attached to Black Stag, and there's a part of me reluctant to ascend because of my love for her. Ascending would mean releasing her for another soul to share and utilize during their time of need, as she did with me. Learning patience, I understood the necessity of letting go of Black Stag because someone else would require her assistance, just as I did, needing protection.

There were several incidents on my way to school and even on the way home where I accidentally hurt myself, and she was there as an aid, helping and healing me. It seemed as though I learned more about myself during my time in higher learning school. It taught me to take the high road. We had tests, several tests to be exact, on how to attack, when to attack, when not to attack, and formations with Archangel Michael. If we weren't in shape when we started, we were by the end of the school season.

Chapter 6
Graduating from Higher Learning Academy

The time was approaching, finally and patiently, for me to complete the higher learning academy. At the end of graduation, Archangel Michael will be selecting six of his top students to work with him and train with him on his army and develop their skills even further to serve in the Sacred Land of Harts.

The training is intense, but so worth it to do because of the things you may or may not ever encounter on your path, you will already be prepared and skilled for, if the time ever arrives. I prefer not to be confrontation, but when being approached with it, his techniques work flawlessly and effectively so far and I plan to use them if I ever have to. In order to be selected as the six, you will have to be able to do a play-by-play of everything that was taught and do it in the field. The last six standing would be selected.

This test was the longest test to take in the field and the hardest because there were a lot of us, but it would prove that I am worthy of earning bigger wings in the end and that's all I could think about. I also couldn't get that formation and all the strategic plans we made during class out of my head. It was like second nature for me now, and it all goes back to the day in middle school that I spinned the wheel of destiny, that I'm here in the first place.

After hours and hours on the field, we finally had the top six, and I was a part of it. Hard work paid off. Upon completion, the top six received their signed and sworn paperwork to begin working with Archangel Michael, along with their completion paperwork. I was excited. I haven't received my bigger wings yet, but well on my way with patience and I still had my black Stag for a little while longer, so I was overjoyed.

Chapter 7
Mentorship with Archangel Michael

It is the first day of work, and I'm excited because I have completed basic school knowledge to perform real soul duties in the Sacred Land of Harts. I didn't realize that I would have to work so closely with souls that lived in the town who were just everyday citizens.

Part of my job included working directly under Archangel Michael's orders in battle and in the town. It was so quiet in the town sometimes, that it made my job a bit boring. I would often ask for extra training with Archangel Michael when he was free to do so during our downtime to keep my skills fresh because I wasn't using them as often.

Most of my job, when not in the town, required me to spend a lot of time at the courthouse, where the highest and last judge you wanted to see was Spirit. If you were going up against judgment against Spirit, you did the highest crime of any soul in the land. We had a few other Judges, but they only looked into lower-level crimes and the punishment and sentencing was a lot less harsh.

The first week of my new job duties, I ran across former classmates, Lucifer and Lilith. They both worked in the area where souls that were punished were held. They oversaw them and made sure they didn't try to escape and that they finished their sentence. I wasn't surprised that this was their duty because they were good souls and even better angels.

I realized after seeing so many souls behind bars, that the town wasn't as pure as I thought, and that my job was much needed to keep it safe. Many good angels were kicked out of the Sacred Land of Harts for being disobedient and why Archangel Michael had us work so hard in the first place because anything can happen with the angels. Their strength is unmatched sometimes.

The experience the first week with Archangel Michael made me realize that there were still many things I have not learned about law, so I decided to go to law school to represent those souls behind bars that cannot speak for themselves.

Chapter 8
Enrolling in the Great School of Sacred Hart

I enrolled in law school the same day I decided I wanted to. It took a little time for my enrollment because I had to be in my job duty for a certain period before applying for more schooling, but that was okay. I still had to do my current duties along with what I was signing up for.

Many of the souls behind bars were there for no reason at all, and after speaking with a few, I knew I needed to speak on their behalf to ensure they weren't being punished for someone else's crime. Some were there because they chose not to spin the wheel of fortune or destiny. They wanted to lead carefree lives and decide their own fate, while others had indeed committed crimes, bringing harm to others.

Listening to their stories motivated me even more to become a lawmaker and try to enact new laws to prevent innocent people from being incarcerated. After a while, I was finally enrolled in law school. I learned everything there was to know about the field, and now I wanted to be of service to those in the courtroom.

Law school took a while to complete, but it was so worth it. Every chance I got, I pleaded with Spirit to consider changing some of the laws in the land. In some cases, He took my considerations into account, and in others, it was a flat-out no. He replied that the rules in place are to protect everyone, and He wouldn't put all my souls at risk to protect just one soul. Of course, I understood.

I haven't finished school yet, but my ambitious nature intimidated all the other law enforcement. I could feel the evil eye of many in the Sacred Land of Harts because some of my efforts have improved the law system, something many of them have tried to do for some time but were unable to succeed. Given the evil eye gave me more fuel for my fire and motivated me to go harder at what I was doing because it means it's working.

Chapter 9
Completing Sacred Law School

The time was drawing near when I was about to complete Law School, a milestone long overdue. Balancing my work with Archangel Michael and attending law school simultaneously demanded a tremendous amount of effort and hard work, but I am immensely grateful that I persevered. Now, I am tasked with taking the bar exam to be accepted as an attorney at law.

Preparing for this exam proved to be more challenging than any other exam I have ever encountered in my academic journey. There are those who hope for my failure, perhaps to deter me from practicing law or to shake my resolve in aiding the souls I have tirelessly worked to save from incarceration. Some have even expressed this sentiment directly to me, saying, "I hope you fail that exam." However, whether I pass or fail, I am resolute in my determination to persist until success is achieved, fueled by their doubt and negativity to propel me forward in my mission to assist others.

Just before I embarked on taking the bar exam, Archangel Michael intercepted me to offer guidance. He asked if I remembered the feelings before and after spinning the wheel on the Wheel of Fortune and how it led me to this moment. He reassured me that some things may not be immediately clear but will eventually make sense. Reminding me that the Creator knows me best and desires what is ultimately best for me. I acknowledged his words, affirming that I indeed recalled those moments and expressed gratitude for his timely reminder.

On the day of the exam, my former classmates from grade school rallied around me, offering their unwavering support and encouragement. They gathered to pray for me at the temple, alongside my own prayers for success. The overwhelming display of love and solidarity on that day was profoundly touching and served as a source of strength as I entered the examination room. With their encouragement and divine guidance, I confidently faced the exam and emerged triumphant, passing with flying colors.

Chapter 10
The Great Divide

Not long after I passed my bar exam, I noticed a difference in the community and how they responded to each other. I decided to go to the temple and speak with the priest, most high, and asked him to pray with me and meditate with me to unite the Land of Sacred Harts.

There was a major divide among us that was starting to get out of control. Souls were starting to form rebellious acts all around and even some of the law enforcements were involved, and it made it much more difficult to enforce the law of the land when there were so many of law enforcements hiding behind the scenes encouraging bad behavior.

It had gotten to the point where you couldn't trust anyone and you had to only rely on intuition. The acts had gotten so bad in the city, that Archangel Michael, Priest most high, and myself decided to protect the citizens of the land by moving them into a much safer environment, small groups at a time, to keep them all from getting hurt.

Darkness had invaded our land and now the time was drawing near that all the training I had done previously with Archangel Michael would have to be used. Souls were protesting to have free will at the way they wanted to live professionally in the Land of Sacred Harts and the angels, even some promoted wanted to do something totally different.

All of those options were something our land provided without the divide, but some took more time than others and spirit always knew our greatest desires way before we ever did, but yet, everyone's perception was different, and some didn't want to put in the work or the time, so instead, a great war began.

Chapter 11
Spiritual War

I never thought I would ever see the day that a war would break out in such a sacred land, the place that's been so good to me, my homeland, and now being destroyed in the blink of an eye by angels and souls.

I was really surprised that two of my classmates, top students of the class, Lucifer and Lilith were involved. They released all the dark forces in the underworld in our land and fought against me instead of with me this time.

I guess Spirit always knew this day would come because of the way he had us trained. I hadn't receive my wings like my other classmates, but I fought this war just as hard. My heart was in pieces at the time I fought because I lost comrades to the other side and my home was being destroyed.

All I could think was that all the work I did to protect souls in the courtroom were for nothing if I had to end up fighting on the battlefield anyway. Angels had fallen from grace and so did souls when this fight was over and done with. I gave everything I had in this war.

Germain and I teamed up along with Archangel Michael for that final blow. When we were done, All the angels that fell to the earth destroyed it as they fell. All the angels that were destroyed soul could not be destroyed. Their souls lurked the earth and they were bound by spirit to do as he ordered as punishment to be responsible for the underworld.

That was the job no one wanted, but two of my best classmates souls were ordered to do so, whether they wanted to or not. Their souls showed Spirit that the underworld is where they wanted to spend eternity and my heart was hurt by it, hurt by all of it.

When I took my last blow, I fell to the ground and was out for a while. Gabriel and Angela worked on me until I finally opened my eyes, and that's when I learned of everything that happen. All I could think of next is now what, what can I do?

Chapter 12
Becoming Human

When I finally regained my strength, I resolved to assist with the cleanup efforts in the Land of Sacred Harts. Time passed, and progress was evident. Spirit was engrossed in a significant project that piqued my curiosity; perhaps it would align with my interests. Germain, Angela, and Gabriel shared my intrigue. However, Chloe opted to focus on completing her current task before the onset of war; she seemed intent on keeping herself occupied, perhaps to distract from thoughts of Lucifer. Their past relationship weighed on my mind, and I silently wished her success in her endeavors, as did we all.

Spirit's project remained shrouded in mystery to most, with only Priest Most High privy to its details. Upon its completion, Archangel Michael and Priest Most High revealed its nature to us: they sought volunteers to assume human form while retaining their angelic abilities and souls, effectively living as they would in the Land of Sacred Harts.

What was left of my class from pre-school onwards are all wanting to volunteer, including myself. Archangel Michael shared that we were from the same soul family, the reason we were all grouped together as kids and all the way through school. I'm the only one from my class that never got promoted to a bigger set of wings and because of that, I was likely not to remember much about my life before migrating to Earth. The vibrational level changes and is much more dense, so I would have to work 10 times harder to obtain my gifts and use them properly.

Archangel Michael then asked, "Do you want to get your wings first before volunteering?" My reply was, "I can do this and I can never forget who I truly am," and so we proceeded. Priest Most High wanted to send us off as couples in union, using our soul names and Earth names. Saint Germain kept his name and added an "E" at the end of it to have it be pronounced the same but spelled differently; my name went from Ariel to Ashley. We became Germaine and Ashley Star. Gabriel became Gary, and Angela became Kayla, and together they became Gary and Kayla Hermit.

We were about to set out, but before I did, before we did, we said goodbye to the land, and I said goodbye to Black Stag. I never got a chance to release her from me because I haven't gotten my wings, but I asked her to protect the land as I would until I return. We both shed a tear and walked away. We left with only the resources we would need to start a life and a family. We were all on to our new journey.

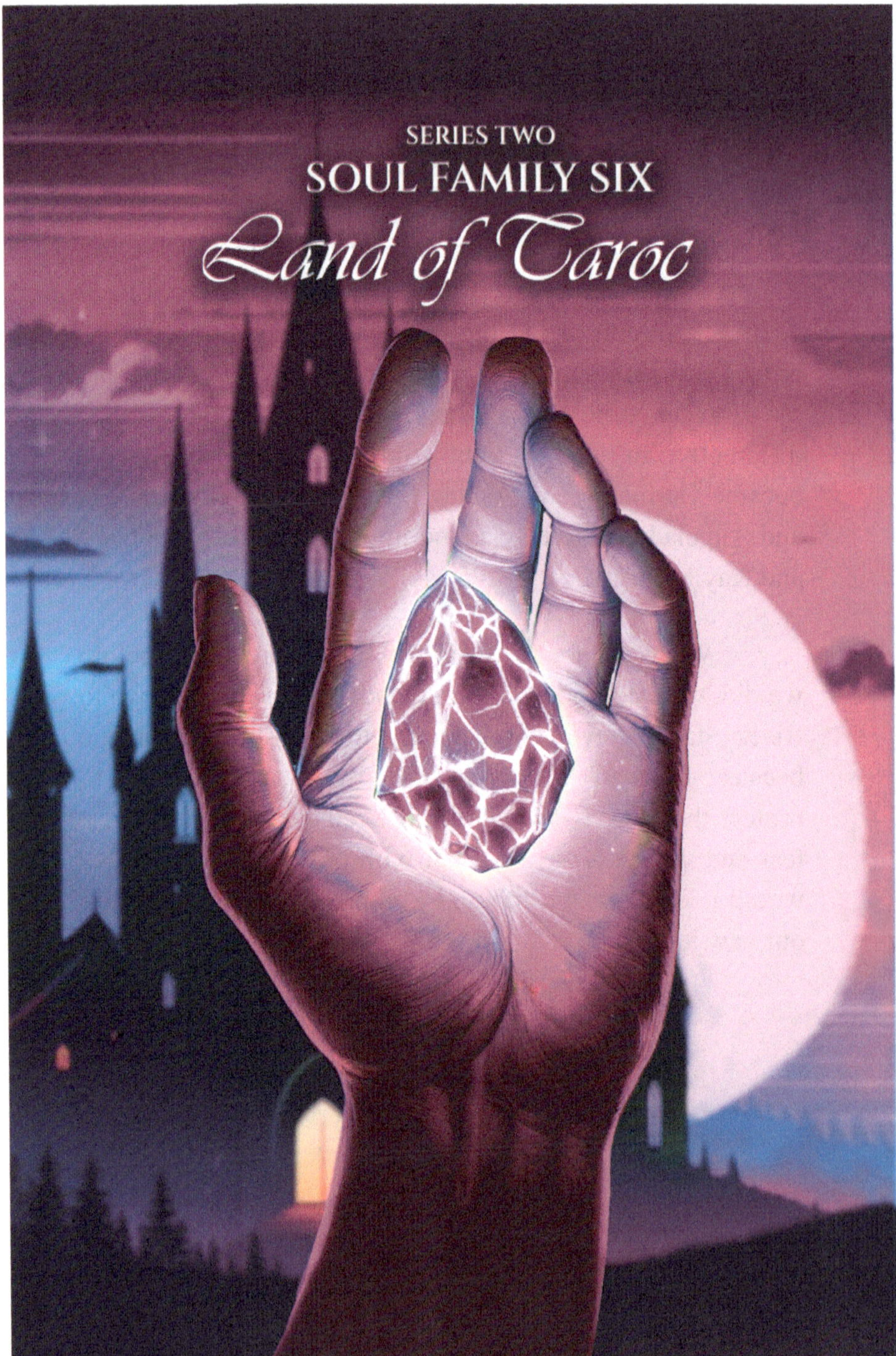
SERIES TWO
SOUL FAMILY SIX
Land of Taroc

SERIES TWO
SOUL FAMILY SIX
Land of Taroc

SUMMARY

Four classmates, Ariel (Lady Ashley), Germain (lord Germaine), Gabriel (lord Gary), and Angela (lady Kayla), from the same soul family create their own land from an Experiment offered by Spirit to become human, in which, will become the greatest land of them all. They all were from soul family six and changed their created names when becoming human and started a family. Ariel (Ashley Star) and Germain (Germaine Star) were married and became the Star family and had four boys, Aries Star (emperor), Taurus Star (King of Coins), Leo Star (King of Fire), Pluto Star (King of Cups), and Uranus Star (King of Swords). Gabriel (Gary Hermit) and Angela (Kayla Hermit), were married and had four girls, Sag Hermit (Sag Star), April Hermit (April Star), August Hermit (August Star), June Hermit (June Star) and Venus Hermit (Venus Star),that eventually married into the Star family. When Lucifer and Lilith discovered Germain and Ariel took on the experiment, they targeted them, their land, and their family for revenge.

Seven newly discovered soul students—Germain, Gabriel, Lucifer, Lilith, Chloe, Angela, and Ariel—embarked on their journey together as classmates, from preschool to higher education. They soon realized they were gifted and more accomplished than most in The Land of Sacred Harts, facing rigorous tests at a very young age. Ariel, the class's most compassionate soul, struggled amidst her peers but eventually found her strength and purpose. However, her newfound resolve was put to the ultimate test when she had to confront her classmates, Lucifer and Lilith, in battle. With the support of her former classmates—Saint Germain (her true love and friend), Gabriel, Angela, and Chloe, who faced her own challenge due to her affection for Lucifer—Ariel braced herself for the ordeal ahead.

Drawing inspiration from the tarot, four classmates migrated from the Land of Sacred Harts. Ariel (Lady Ashley Star), Saint Germain (Lord Germaine Star), Gabriel (Lord Gary Hermit), and Angela (Lady Kayla Hermit)—souls of angels, with Ariel being the one with the heart of an angel, though never fully manifesting her larger wings. Lady Ashley Star (Ariel), volunteering from soul family six to experience humanity, started a family alongside former classmates: Saint Germain (Lord Germaine Star), Angela (Lady Kayla Hermit), and Gabriel (Lord Gary Hermit). Together, they raised children—Aries Star (Emperor), Sag Hermit Star (Empress), Taurus Star (King of Coins), April Hermit Star (Queen of Coins), Leo Star (King of Fire), August Hermit Star (Queen of Fire), Pluto Star (King of Cups), June Hermit Star (Queen of Cups), Uranus Star

(King of Swords), and Venus Hermit Star (Queen of Swords). They built a powerful land prophesied by Archangel Michael, fulfilling their destiny after establishing their family there.

In the construction of this great land, shadowy forces mysteriously invaded, and the truth behind the chaos dawned upon all: it was none other than their former classmates, Lucifer and Lilith, who had turned rebellious in the Sacred Land of Harts. As younger siblings to Archangel Michael, they sought revenge on their former peers for their imprisonment and servitude in the underworld, punishment inflicted upon them by the land.

Aries, thought to have returned from the grave, had never truly perished. He had been strategically employed as bait, luring out the enemy to safeguard his home and kin. The Star family understood that Lucifer and Lilith would stop at nothing to besmirch all they had toiled for. Thus, the real Aries and his kin remained concealed in the town adjacent to the village throughout. Instead of summoning them, a messenger owl arrived to forewarn them of Lucifer and Lilith's scheme and advise them to remain in place.

Collaboratively, the Hermits and Star parents devised an illusion to ensnare their former classmates, mirroring the methods used against them. With the threat neutralized—or so they believed—the Star children embarked on new beginnings, each starting families of their own. Yet, unbeknownst to them, Lucifer and Lilith, upon learning of their former classmates' impending grandchildren, recognized the ruse and conspired to launch another assault, enlisting aid from external forces.

Chapter 13
Land of Creation

Long, long ago, in a faraway land, was a land known to no one, no life force, no anything, until two people on a quest for knowledge and wisdom of who they are and what their life meant decided to make that land their home. Their names were Germaine and Ashley Star, recently married with carrying only everything they own on their back. They were from a very sacred land, the Land of Hart, and wanted to know what it was like to live a life outside of that land, so They built a small town in that unknown land, starting a family and building from the ground up with what little they had for resources.

The land was quite big, but because it was so few of them, they only utilized a small portion of that space, dreaming of the day they could grow it into a place everyone wanted to live. The family of two grew to a family of seven, with the two having five boys: Aries, Taurus, Leo, Pluto and Uranus. They all had different responsibilities, with Aries being the most responsible one since he was the oldest. The parents, Germaine and Ashley, were very curious people and discovered that during their quest for knowledge, that they were from Soul Family Six. They were the most caring people and loved their home and family deeply. They were also very generous with other lands, with the limited resources they had.

They learned of their soul path right before discovering the Land of Taroc from their teacher,

Archangel Michael, who was a spiritual being who approached them right before discovering the land to inform them of who they were, what they were chosen to do and why. He shared with them that they were to take on human form and take human names instead of using the names they were created with, except Germaine, he kept his name, and that they were to start a family because of their nurturing spirit and caring souls and also build a home of their own in a land up ahead because that land would become a great nation one day.

Germaine and Ashley, giving up her name as Ariel until their assignment ends, did just that, started and raised their family of boys. Aries, the oldest son, had a heart full of passion, was fearless, and was a natural-born leader; Taurus loved finer things and beauty but was very practical and dependable when you needed him to be; Leo was fierce and confident like his brother Aries, but loved living his life to the fullest instead just living and being in charge at home, Uranus was the thinker and innovator of the family, always thinking of a more simpler way to do things for the benefit of self and others and Pluto was the mysterious child, and the youngest.

He's very compassionate and empathetic towards others despite the mystery. In another city, in the Land of Taroc, was another Soul Family from six. The family had five girls, the same age as Aries, Taurus, Leo, Uranus, and Pluto. Their names were Sag, April, August, June, and Venus. Their parents were Gary and Kayla Hermit, a very quiet family and also good friends from the sacred land of

Harts, who also married the same day as Germaine and Ashley on their quest.

They often visited each family's town to help their children grow and evolve from one another. The parents of each family learned from each other as well, and the families became closer. Since there were more families migrating from the Sacred Land of Harts from Soul Family Six, they all migrated to the Land of Taroc to be with their soul group. There were also other lands among them that had other Soul Families migrate, but they lived differently from Soul Family Six, but sacred just the same. One night while everyone was asleep, Ashley received a message to prepare her family for great destruction to come across the land in waves from an angelic being.

It was to happen in series over time and to prepare her family and the town for it as much as possible and as soon as possible. During this same time, Aries and Sag were courting, and he asked for her hand in marriage, and she happily replied yes. Ashley held off on telling her boys right away what happened because of Aries's great news to wed, but she shared the news with Germaine, and they planned accordingly without revealing a lot to the boys about what was going to happen in an unknown time. Since there were so many people in the land now, a certain order and laws had to be put in place, especially with the news Ashley received from the angelic being.

After the wedding ceremony for Aries and Sag, another ceremony took place crowning them the Emperor and Empress of the land, the authority figures who would be in control of people out of order and lay down the law in the Land of Taroc. Ashley and Germaine passed their crowns to their oldest son and his new wife. Later that year, Taurus asked April to marry him, and she happily said yes. They had been courting as long as Aries and Sag and loved one another very much, so within the week, they too were married and crowned to their own town in the land of Taroc called the Land of Coins, where they created the life they wanted, but still preparing for a destruction that wasn't visible to the naked eye and one they still weren't told about.

Chapter 14
Town of Coins

The town of Coins was filled with items created by citizens that were considered luxury items, with Taurus and his new wife, April, overseeing what came in and out of that town and what could be sold there. Anyone that was anyone wanted to live in the land of coins. Lady Ashley and Lord Germaine, along with Lady Kayla and Lord Gary and Aries and wife Sag, lived in this prestigious living establishment. Uranus was responsible for how everything was built concerning all construction in every town, so many lived in his town as well because he had such a brilliant mind. Although Lady Ashley and Lord Germaine gave up their crowns, they still are the most powerful in the land and work in secret with Archangel Michael, their childhood teacher, to ensure everyone's safety, including the emperor and empress. Lady Ashley cloaked all the wardrobes of her family and their crowns to protect them from dark entities without them even knowing it. Although the emperor and empress have gifts, their gifts are intensified with the cloak of Lady Ashley.

She especially wanted to keep an eye on her son Taurus because he oftentimes got distracted by money and greed and dark entities looking for a way in, and while she kept an eye on the entire Land, putting a cloak over the entire area, Lord Germaine was ordered to go undercover to other towns and cities to investigate their behaviors to see if dark entities had come into those cities as an unknown citizen or taken over the bodies of citizens. Lady Ashley made him appear as a citizen, and Lord Germaine took the sword made by his son to detect darkness in the land by any man, animal, or thing. Because Lady Ashley could see and have visions through any mirror or reflection, she was able to track Lord Germaine, plus she could be in many places at once with her teleportation.

She often used owls to keep watch and report to her a threat or danger in the land. One particular night, in the town of coins, an unknown figure or dark entity appeared in Lady Ashley's vision, and before it could find a source or body to hide in, she destroyed it immediately. She never told her family she received a message directly from an angelic being, other than to Lord Germaine, that there would actually be destruction from dark entities; she only shared to always be prepared for anything and stay alert.

Chapter 15
The Town of Fire

The town of Fire was governed by Leo and his new wife, August. They wedded weeks before accepting their roles in town. They were crowned by their parents just like their other siblings who were married before them. The town was created beautifully, and there were so many warm-hearted people who lived there and were so welcoming. Leo and August made sure that every town and city had supplies to cook with and stay warm with by keeping wood stocked all over, and they used all the knights in the town to get it done more quickly. Lady Ashley was having visions about what happened prior to incarnating about the great war that happened in the Land of Sacred Hart and who was responsible for it, and intuitively, she felt Lucifer and his sister Lilith could be responsible for the dark entities appearing randomly, but could not prove it yet.

Waiting on an update from Lord Germaine on his findings, but in the meantime, she worked with all the pages in every town and city to prepare them for the unknown and put a plan together with all the leaders to cover the homes they all built together. The town of fire was also known for its passions and desires. Most of the citizens that lived in town were very driven and optimistic about making their home lives better and those around them. In a way, Lady Ashley connected more with the town of fire because her passion is what led her to the path she was currently on.

Chapter 16
The Town of Cups

The town of Cups was probably the most creative land to live in and the place where a lot of things were created and made. Pluto and his wife, Venus, newly married managed all the ins and outs of this town. They married weeks before they were crowned for their duties in town. They worked perfectly together in managing day to day to day activities, but they lacked the skills of the Emperor, Aries, and Empress Sag when it came to detecting dark entities in the environment, but very intuitive when it came to people's emotions. Lady Ashley knew all too well what the capabilities were of dark forces and how far they would go to tap into the energies of the weak at their most vulnerable state, especially through a town full of water that many drank from. Empress Sag ordered the pages that were old enough to be out at night to take turns watching all the main sources and outlets of water in not only the town of Cups but in all the Land of Taroc. She had her suspicions, and so did Aries.

There were pettier disagreements and arguments in the town of Cups to make everyone suspicious, too many to count, when it's very peaceful in other towns. Lord Germaine astro-projected a message to Lady Ashley that their trouble in other lands, but that he could not go into details about where he was and that a messenger owl was on its way with what was found. Aries and Sag are now coming up with a plan to protect the townsmen from themselves, especially in the town of Cups. The Emperor,

Aries, and Empress, Sag, decided to have Uranus and his wife develop a tool that could detect poison in all the towns before any water could be used in any way to protect everyone there. They temporarily built a small area for each family on the outside of the Land of Taroc in tents and borrowed bare necessities from other towns until everything had been tested and cleared for living. It took a few days, but everything was tested and cleared for living.

Chapter 17
The Town of Swords

There was a leadership meeting being held in the town of Swords. This is the town where all the structural plans and all the weapons are created by Uranus and his wife, Venus. They had been married a while but recently stepped into the leadership role together in the town of Swords. Aries and Sag called a meeting alerting everyone that they would need all hands on deck or younger pages to volunteer for training in the field with Aries and Lady Ashley in case there would be an invasion in towns. They wanted to be prepared as much as possible for the unknown due to the unsettling message that Lady Ashley received from Lord Germaine.

Lady Ashley took other measures to get information quicker by sending all her owl connections into each town that Lord Germaine had not been to yet and sending a message to him to come home so he could help prepare an army. Somehow, Lady Ashley and Sag both knew that something was coming. They gathered up all the Queens and had them prepare all the female pages to help the wounded, along with Kayla and Gary, who were very good at healing work. Lady Ashley did a head count in every town and asked Uranus to create a weapon that detect dark forces to sell to every family that wanted it to protect their homes and families. A really big decision needed to be made by the Emperor and Empress at this point, and that was if they wanted to ask for help from allied Soul Families to take down dark forces together or to try this individually as a town and Land.

It was risky asking for help because the talk of the town was that dark forces had already reached other lands, and if we asked for help, would that dark force be among them, and would we be calling in the dark forces. Lady Ashley thought they should wait to make that decision until after Lord Germaine returned, but it was the Emperor and Empress's decision.

Chapter 18
Completion of the Lands

Lord Germaine arrived back in the land of Taroc, along with the messenger owls with intel from other lands, but before he had returned, The Emperor and Empress had already decided to come together with the other Soul Families to meet about the darkness that caused subtle changes in each town's environment. What Lord Germaine and the messenger owls had to say was devastating, to say the least. Each Soul Family was plotting to destroy the other Soul Families working with them up close, learning the ins and outs of each land to overthrow them to prove that their Soul Family was the best and stroke their ego-boosting about it. Soul Family Six was not about to let that happen.

Aries and Sag traveled by chariot to meet in the middle of another land, and of course, Lady Ashley was going to make her presence known by sending a messenger owl to watch, and she saw through the eyes of the owl while Lord Germaine traveled with them. Someone had to stay in the Land of Taroc to protect the land from invaders and no one could really do that better than Lady Ashley. She had eyes everywhere. Once everyone arrived in the middle, they rested for a day and met the next morning to talk about a strategy to protect each land from dark forces. Aries and Sag seem to be the most concerned about the darkness that was plaguing our land, but most other families were there to see how they could work together with each Soul Family to gain financial wealth in each land.

Aries replied, each land is doing very well financially, so why would we need to combine everything now when the biggest issues are the fighting and the arguments that have increased over all the lands that seem to be unsettling. In their eye, that was nothing. Greed was starting to consume them, and at this point, the meeting was over for Aries and Sag. They were on their own in how they could protect their land from chaos, but our neighboring lands were starting to have great influence over Soul Family Six.

Chapter 19
Times of Destruction and Chaos

Arguments and fights began to grow stronger and stronger in all the lands causing action to be made right away. Lady Ashley made it a point to find the source of the problem. These dark forces weren't coming from nowhere, and she felt that intuitively. Before making The Land of Taroc their home, Lady Ashley thought back to the time when they were about to move their very vaguely. She remembers Archangel Michael saying that because the vibration of this land is so dense, you may not remember who you were and all of your abilities, not even your real name and that you would have to call on Spirit to get the answers you seek. You will feel like your old life was just a dream, and you may even remember others, but you may not quite remember how. You will still have your gifts and can use them, but you will have to have an inner knowing inside of you on how to use them.

Lady Ashley was ready to try anything at this point to protect her land. She called on Spirit and asked, can you reveal to me the unseen that was seen in a previous time and space to protect my land, our land. Spirit heard her loud and clear and showed her only what she should see right now. She saw that she was a natural-born warrior who moved with great determination, and now she was ready to put a plan together with Lord Germaine, Aries, Taurus, Uranus, and Pluto.

She asked Lady Kayla to work with all the Queens and the Empress on preparing all the female pages for battle, Lord Gary, along with Lord Germaine, worked with all the male pages, and Lady Ashley worked with the knights for battle. The town didn't have much time to prepare but did what they could. Lady Ashley is the magician, so she cast a spell to remove all the citizens in the Land of Taroc immediately to the safe shelter built in the unseen under her spell when the battle began.

She felt intuitively that it was going to happen based on what Spirit shared. The dark forces were destroying all the other lands around the Land of Taroc but paled in comparison to the messenger owls reported from other Soul Families. It was time to put all our plans in action, but there was one thing Lady Ashley knew she had to do that she had the ability to do. Call in reinforcements.

Chapter 20
Calling in Reinforcements

Lady Ashley knew that if she could call on anyone, she could call on Archangel Michael for help and support during this dark time for answers. He appeared to her in the mirror of truth, and she cried to him, Archangel Michael, we need your help. All the lands have become corroded with dark forces beyond our control, including my very own. My family and I have put together a plan to try to avoid a battle but also prepared for one in case a peaceful resolution could not be had. Please step in if you can to help us overcome this peacefully and amicably. He replied, I will do what I can or what Spirit will allow me to do. I'll be there with you for sure in spirit because you are from my army, but you have this. He also replied, I have seen you fight, and you were the last soul standing, not only for what was right. After having this talk with Archangel Michael, she moved with great determination and she knew that she could face anything and she had a whole family behind her. There was a rumor that a different group of Soul Families were traveling their way to the Land of Taroc to wreak havoc, and the messenger owls confirmed it. It was time to put our plan into action. Didn't appear from the way they were charging towards us that this would be peaceful, but we are not going down without a fight, Lady Ashley replied.

Chapter 21
The Great Battle of Soul Families

Other Soul Families had reached our land, but they didn't get very far. There were traps all over town that Uranus built with his brothers; some you could and some you couldn't see with the human eye. For some, it ended before it started, especially in the town of Swords. Lady Ashley safely transported all the elderly citizens and small children with her spell, placing them somewhere safe during this battle. At every turn, the other Soul Families tried to invade the land, but their attempts were blocked. A real fight took several hours to even immense because there were so many illusions cast by Soul Family Six to protect not only the people in the land, but the land itself. The other Soul Families were tiring, which was the plan anyway, to have them tire out. They were surprised by our attacks and what we were able to do and underestimated our strategies.

They were beginning to doubt their own abilities because they wanted to be the best and even began fighting each other. The fight was getting out of hand, and Lady Ashley and Lord Germaine asked for a resolution to be made to end this petty fight and began to ask them why the fight started in the first place. Aries and Sag brought up the force of darkness, reminding them that this was the true cause of the fight and asked if they would join forces with them instead of against them to keep darkness from our lands. They all agreed and all decided to help with efforts of restoring each other's land with balance and harmony once again. The battle was over, but the real one had yet to begin.

Chapter 22
Rest and Recuperate

After all the clean-up efforts for each land that took a while to rebuild, we can finally rest and enjoy our homes again without feeling like something could happen at any moment. Things could happen at any moment, but just for a moment, we wanted to rest our minds and bodies from so much overall in the last weeks and months. Lord Germaine ordered more rest for Aries because he sustained the most injuries from the battle. Taurus, Uranus, Pluto, and Leo suffered injuries as well, but small in comparison to Aries. Most of the clean-up efforts came from the citizens in town, and all people who fought on the frontlines were ordered by Lord Germaine and Lady Ashley to rest properly and not overload with work right away because they may need their strength sooner than they knew.

The Star family and Hermit family decided to go and rest where they previously rested during the testing of all the towns to be sure no one lifted a finger and got proper rest without worry. Sag was really concerned about Aries's health, and she asked if Lady Ashley and her mom, Lady Kayla, could help her in healing him so he would be a full strength again. They did the healing work, but they also had an alternate plan for their family, and it was for their protection. The Star Family and Hermit Family were asked to stay a little longer where they were and to return home once a messenger owl alerted them. They all agreed.

The messenger owl that would come would be one they had never seen before, and it would be able to speak fully in understanding, and if one was to come and it didn't speak, it would be an imposter. The family agreed to stay behind. Deep down, they all knew that the fight that would be fought next would be one they may not be able to survive.

Chapter 23
Peace to all Lands

There was finally peace in all the lands. The Soul Families as a group decided that they no longer wanted to live in such a divided land by Soul Families. The deal was if anyone wanted to live in any land, they could, and we happily agreed that if Soul Families wanted to move and live outside of their Soul Families, they could if they so desired. It was time for us to grow and evolve and also learn from each other different skill sets to become better as humans. There was peace to the lands a long while before darkness began to sneak back in. The Star and Hermit family returned, the entire family, to the Land of Taroc in full strength, ready to fulfill their duties in the role they were given in the town where they lived.

When they all returned, the peace was felt, but deep down, no one was comfortable knowing that darkness was still among them. Everyone could feel it, even the animals and small pages. The Emperor and Empress decided that everyone could use some fun, so they decided to plan a huge gathering and included all the other nations if they wanted to participate in some fun, food, and games in town to lighten the mood and give everyone hope again that their homes were safe. All the other Soul Families agreed that this would be good for morale, and they planned a full week of fun all day for five days.

Everyone enjoyed themselves and agreed it was much needed and hoped to do it again real soon. They all came to each other's towns and enjoyed each activity of games and fun the way they do it in their town, they helped other lands try new things as well.

Chapter 24
Dark Entity in our Mist Returns

Lady Ashley, Lady Kayla, Lord Germaine, and Lord Gary had the same senses when it came to dark forces in their mist. It's likely because they were formal classmates together in Land of Sacred Harts, and they were sensing their other classmates had fallen from grace. Lady Ashley can only sense things, but the rest of them know because their vibration and status in the Land of Sacred Harts were higher in ranking; nevertheless, their presence was sensed. Lady Ashley was beginning to remember remnants of her life as Ariel from sensing their presence. Her powers were increasing, not that she wasn't a force already, but her intuition had been heightened. Chloe had come to her in a dream, a former classmate to help her on this part of her journey. She knew what she was about to encounter; all of them, to be exact, would encounter more than they'd already seen.

She warned Lady Ashley and said that she was being heavily protected by her and her family. In that same dream, the Priest was most high, and Archangel Michael promoted her for her bravery with the next level of wings for her soul. She mastered the hardest part of this journey. Lady Ashley awakened, looked over at Lord Germaine, and smiled. She got up and looked out into the world, and she said, Lilith, I know you are out there, and when our paths cross, there will be a debt to pay for all the destruction you caused my family: you and Lucifer both.

As she said it, Lucifer and Lilith both heard in awe that her abilities were strong enough to sense them in the dense land they were in, but her vibrations were increased even higher than her former classmates due to what was yet to come.

Chapter 25
Town of Coins Attack

In the middle of the night, there was a silent attack, the kind no one saw coming, into the town of coins. It was a lot of bickering and going back of forth over things the people in town would not usually get upset about; this is why it was considered silent. No one expected a fight to break out, especially after the fight we had with other Soul Families. Taurus, the King, came out to see what the commotion was about because it was happening near their home. He would usually send a knight out to patrol the area, but it was late and near his window, and it was unusually late. The minute he walked out, the two fighting grabbed him and took him away in a chariot, out of the town, to hold him hostage and take over the land. It threw Taurus off.

All Taurus could think was, who is this, why have they captured me, and would anyone know where to look for him. April, his wife, noticed he was gone longer than usual and began to look for him. When she discovered he was missing, she contacted the Emperor and the Empress, Aries and Sag, alerting them to go out and search for him. Aries said that it might be an ambush to reach others in power by going out this late to look for him and that they would get together during daylight and put a plan together to find him. April angrily agreed. She wanted her husband found immediately, but she also didn't want others getting hurt because they really didn't know what they were up against.

Chapter 26
Town of Fire Attack

Daylight has finally arrived, and Leo, decided they should put together a plan in the town of fire. The Emperor, Aries, King Leo, Pluto, and Uranus all met with the knights in each town to go on a manhunt for King Taurus. They wanted to try to get things done and taken care of without alerting their parents, Lord Germaine and Lady Ashley, but nothing got past them. While they were holding their meeting in a town to be secretive, Lady Ashley already had 2 messenger owls in on their conversation listening to their plan, and she could already sense who was behind Taurus being taken. Lady Ashley had a dream prior to any attacks made about dark forces wanting to destroy what she and her family built, so she took protective measures into her own hands for her entire family.

She knows wherever Taurus is, he's untraceable. She had Uranus design a device to be able to find them anywhere at any time that she could sense. She could not sense him. Lady Ashley and Lord Germaine are heading to the meeting right away to warn their sons to allow them to find him. They are treading into dangerous territories that they may not be able to go up against, but before Lady Ashley and Lord Germaine can reach their sons, dark forces come out of nowhere and attack the town, causing major damage, taking King Leo with them.

Lady Ashley was close enough to them to throw a tracking device on one of the dark forces to lead them to where they were heading and sent a messenger owl to follow and report back. Lord Germaine and Lady Ashley loved their loves and at any point could have defected the forces, but they wanted to find King Taurus and King Leo being taken was the only other way they could see helping get both their sons back.

Chapter 27
Town of Cups Attack

Since there were clean-up efforts in the town of fire from so much damage from an attack, a lot of citizens slept in the other towns that had available space until their homes were rebuilt. The town of Cups was the neighboring town, and so many citizens, including King Pluto and Queen June, were overwhelmed with fear and out of answers to keep the citizens safe because those attacks in each town prior were back to back. Lord Germaine and Ashley decided to build a shelter with the help of all the citizens who were able-bodied in another land nearby, hidden and protected with her magic to protect everyone that was either too old to fight, too young to fight, and those with no training yet in the battlefield, to live there temporarily until a solution could be made to stop the chaos from happening again in the Land of Taroc.

Violence was at an all-time high, and King Pluto and King Uranus, along with Aries, decided to prepare for battle. Pluto and Uranus were still mildly injured, but Aries was in no shape to fight a battle as serious as the one they were about to encounter. Although it was quiet, it seemed to be a little too quiet. The knights and pages should have been preparing for a battle at any time, but for some reason, everyone appeared to be resting or appearing as if they could not keep their eyes open. Lord Germaine ordered everyone not to drink, bathe, or touch water or liquid of any kind because it had been tampered with.

The attack this time was a silent one, causing everyone who drank the water, touched the water, or touched it in the town of Cups to be affected in a way they could not perform. Everyone who could not perform was taken to the hidden shelter at once to seek care and healing at once.

Chapter 28
Sleep and Slumber

Everyone who was affected by the water or liquids in any form slept for days. Whatever dark forces that were among them were coming back to back to where everyone in the Land of Taroc had to seek refuge in other places. The entire town of Cups was asleep, including the King and Queen. Lord Germaine and Lady Ashley had to regroup and wait on a message from the messenger owl before planning a move. They still needed to find King Taurus and Leo. It always seems to be an act of dark forces anytime they try to group together a plan, and it always seems to involve their sons. King Uranus and Emperor Aries are the only ones actually present to help, but at this point, this battle is bigger than them, and Lord Germaine and Lady Ashley ask them to stay out of this one and protect the families at the shelter while they find out what's really going on.

There were people asleep and wasn't waking anytime soon and now they needed to know why and how they could help them regain consciousness. Everything was still unexplainable. While things were quiet at the shelter, things were also quiet where Leo and Taurus were. They were together with no clue as to why they were being held captive in a place where they were free to walk and roam, but with no way out, no exit or sign of entry. The messenger owl finally reached where they were but was puzzled as to how anyone would get in or out of where they were.

The messenger could sense both of their energies but had no way to see them or get in where they were. The messenger is now heading back to report its findings, and while that is happening, Leo and Taurus try to think like their brother, Uranus, and find their way out.

Chapter 29
Investigations of Lord Germaine

Lord Germaine decided to investigate these attacks in other areas to see if their family and land were being targeted or if this was happening all over. He disguised himself as a citizen. Lady Ashley made him appear differently and changed it so that he could not be sensed by darkness before he got where he was going. He was prepared to be gone a while with plenty of fresh fruit and food vitamins for vitality as he traveled. He didn't pack water with him because some parts of it were unsafe, and they hadn't had time to undo what had been done to tarnish it before he left, so he will get some on the way in another town and test it with what Uranus made to show whether it was safe or unsafe to drink or touch.

Uranus built that especially for his dad for his travels, but built something much bigger for the town so that they could get back to how they lived before. Everything was moving forward slowly but with optimism. Lady Ashley kissed Lord Germaine on his way out and said, I love you. Be safe and. I will be able to see everything you see with the tracker you have on you, and I will be able to help you when you need help as you travel. He kissed her back and was on his way. As he was on his way, he ran into the messenger owl. The owl recognized Lady Ashley's cloak and stopped Lord Germaine from conveying a message about where her sons were. And Lady Ashley translated it to Lord Germaine, and he followed the owl. He moved in quietly and investigated the area and, how to get in and how to get out.

Once Lord Germaine was able to sense his sons, he asked Lady Ashley to teleport them all back to where she was, and so she did. Once she was able to sense them all, she was able to bring them all back safely and quietly to the hidden shelter for the town.

Chapter 30
Lucifer and Lilith Behind the Darkness

Because Lord Germaine did not spend much time investigating before finding his sons, he decided to go back out and do more investigating to get the truth of what was happening and to help the Land of Taroc thrive again. Lady Ashley lent her support again because this was nothing like what they had truly encountered, and they were unable to see the true enemy, so they combined their powers to trace down the real root of the problem and how it could be resolved. He disguised himself yet again. He discovered that what other Soul Families were experiencing was mild in comparison to what was happening in the Land of Taroc, but as he looked closer to the behavior of a few of the other Soul Families, a lot of the citizens appeared to be motionless and unaware of their surroundings. Lord Germaine tested his theory by asking questions to a few of the citizens, and his theory was right, but there was one in Soul Family Five's town that was playing along to fit in until he noticed Lord Germaine, and they both discovered each other. Paul noticed Lord Germaine wasn't behaving like the other citizens, and he pulled him in and explained to him what he suspected was going on. It threw Lord Germaine off slightly, but nevertheless, he was happy to see at least one person who appeared to be in awareness, but he was also suspicious, and so was Lady Ashley. She could feel and sense everything that was happening, and they were also connecting telepathically, and any suspicion he had, Lady Ashley's, was heightened.

Chapter 31
Land of Illusions

Lady Ashley and Lord Germaine have high sensitivity to their senses, but when they are linked together, they become even stronger, and they both sensed the same thing, and it's heightened. They both realized that you had to be of strong forces to sense or recognize them in the midst of them being undercover, and they realized the person they were speaking to was either like them or working with dark forces. Lady Ashley was miles away but could still sense the presence of danger and warned Lord Germaine that it was likely he was speaking with Lucifer and to proceed with caution. Lord Germaine was already on it and suspected it, so he asked indirect questions to see if he could get answers without Lucifer, disguised as Paul, noticing who he really was.

It was clear to Lord Germaine that no ordinary man would be able to master the strength of a high-level being or dark one without being one themselves. Paul gave the story that he had been traveling and just returned home to see that everyone in town appeared distant and unaware of their surroundings and noticed Lord Germaine seemed to be in the same state of mind as him, which is true, but then Lord Germaine decides to ask, what led to your travel and how long had it been since he left and returned.

Paul replied I left a few days ago to deliver a message for help from other nations from our king in my town because the food supply was getting low, and a lot of people were moving into other lands due to shortage. Lord Germaine then asked again, the same question 2 or 3 more times before he realized he may have been in some sort of time loop. Lucifer, disguised as Paul, was trying to draw Lord Germaine into a trap, but Lady Ashley recognized the trap and teleported him back to the Land of Taroc and not to the safe house because she wasn't sure if it was safe yet for him to return where everyone was. It may jeopardize their safety, so he put on his armor of protection, along with Lady Ashley's white spell, and laid low.

Chapter 32
The Awakening

Everyone that had fallen into a deep slumber was finally awakening. No one remembers a thing, but they all said it was the best sleep they ever had. They had not been able to rest properly since silent attacks started happening all over the Land of Taroc. Everyone had become paranoid and suspicious of everything and everyone and for a brief moment, they had peace of mind. Empress Sag and Emperor Aries wanted them to have peace of mind and informed everyone that they were giving all the efforts they had to ensure that happened. Lady Ashley and Lady Kayla noticed that not only did everyone awake where they were, but everywhere else where people seemed to be unaware of their environment had awakened as well.

They weren't sure if it was from their efforts, if there was a spell broken or if there was something more to come. Either way, they are preparing for the unexpected. Uranus and Venus have been working day and night to build something strong enough to defeat our enemies. With every sword built, Lady Ashley, Lady Kayla, Lord Germaine, and Lord Gary were given the power to create a weapon of mass destruction for dark forces. Only those with godlike powers could defect or go up against something they can't see or touch but sense in energy.

Chapter 33
Town of Swords Attack

There was an attack on the Town of Swords, but this attack was intentional. Everything was destroyed, including all the weapons that were created for war. This was when Lady Ashley realized that this was personal and their every move was being watched. Once she realized they were being watched, she began building a trap to cause an illusion to her enemies about what was really happening to buy some time and throw the enemy off their trail. She sent every messenger in the sky to every town nearby to round up all the resources they had to build a weapon or weapons to destroy their enemy. Lady Ashley realized that the dark forces either were caught in the illusion, or they knew she would be able to hear them even if it was an illusion.

Lilith whispered in her ear that she would find them and destroy her and her whole family once they discovered where they really were. Lady Ashley and Lady Kayla united their powers along with Lord Gary to teleport everyone there safely without being tracked so that they could buy time to destroy Lucifer and Lilith. Their powers and gifts were as strong as their own, so they needed to call in higher forces and move all the citizens as far away from the Land of Taroc as possible. Everyone from other towns brought in everything they had to spare to help aid in this war. This would be even bigger than the one they once had, but it was able to end peacefully.

Chapter 34
Unity of All Great Soul Nations

This is the time when everyone came together more than before to do what is right for the greater good. Almost every sword Uranus and Venus made for other towns and lands was donated back to them for this spiritual war. It gave everyone great joy to see all the members of the Soul Family come together again and join forces, even under these circumstances. It made everyone who could not truly be on the front lines come together and play a role in some way, even if it was in a small way. While everyone was working together, Lady Ashley received a message from Spirit in her waken state; usually, her messages come in her sleep, but this message was important.

Spirit replied You've done well; you and my child have gone above and beyond what I expected, and now you shall receive your rewards. I will restore your memory of who you once were before becoming human and promote you to an Archangel, Ariel. You deserve it, and I will also give you access to White Stag. Lady Ashley cried when she remembered everything about her life before becoming human, but it was tears of joy because she finally got her wings, and it took becoming human to achieve it, which was even harder to accomplish. She happily accepted. Spirit also said that there is another surprise for you, but you will see that on the battlefield soon enough and that I love you, my child.

Chapter 35
Archangel Michael's Army Reunite

Lady Ashley returns back to everyone, and she asks Aries, Sag, Taurus, April, Leo, August, June, Pluto, Uranus and Venus to lead everyone to the safe house area on the outside of the Land of Taroc, where they will all be safe during the war. All the weapons have been made, and now they need to go somewhere safe because they have all been targeted as revenge on Lord Germaine and Gary and also Lady Ashley and Kayla from former classmates; they once destroyed their original homeland or were a part of that destruction. They all know what kind of damage that could be caused by their former classmate, and they all want their children and town's people safe.

They all agreed to lead everyone out, and as they were leading everyone to safety, Archangel Michael appeared and said, it's time. Do you all remember the formations? Emperor Aries looked back and witnessed something he had never seen before and became curious, just as his parents did as toddlers. He followed them out into the battlefield and watched his parents and in-laws transform into their angel forms. He was blown away and impressed at the same time.

Before the battle began, everyone looked around and noticed Ariel's wings were bigger than all of theirs and how powerful she had become. Everyone noticed her increase in power, and now they know where it came from. When Ariel looked to her right, she saw Chloe, another classmate of theirs, who stayed behind to get her wings, and she got them; though they weren't as big as Ariel's, she received them. All of the invisible cages were in place, and everyone had swords that were blessed with the power to suck up any dark forces. Lucifer and Lilith finally showed up, but still in a way of an illusion because they knew that this battle wasn't to be easy.

They, too, noticed that Ariel got wings, which was one of the highest accomplishments to have as an angel. The fighting had begun and they all got in formation as if it never left them, and it didn't. As the fight began, Black Stag flew in and joined the fight. Ariel replied it's good to see your old friend. I didn't think I would still have access to you after I received my wings, Black Stag replied; you were the last one; everyone else went out on assignments, so I will be with you always old friend. They looked at each other, nodded and continued to fight. Lucifer and Lilith continued with the illusion, and every dark force went into the swords so that they could all be released in the underworld jail.

Lucifer noticed Aries watching in the background and called out to Saint Germaine and Ariel, I have your offspring, and now I have my revenge. He took a sword to Aries and took his life. Ariel was in such a rage she finished that battle with the invisible cages and locked them both in it. They didn't see it coming. Ariel and Saint Germaine wept for their son and returned to their human form as Archangel Michael took Lucifer and Lilith back to the underworld. They won the battle, but they lost the war when they lost their son.

Chapter 36
Death of Aries

The victory against Lucifer and Lilith was short-lived for the Star Family. Aries, in the end, became the hero because he was bait to draw out the enemy, but not by choice. The whole Land of Taroc was grieving the loss of a great leader, loving husband, and devoted son to his parents. The death of Aries was one no one expected because he was asked to lead everyone to safety, but yet no one sensed his presence. All the planning to protect everyone and the leader getting killed caused a lot of citizens to lose hope. Lord Germaine and Lady Ashley asked them all not to give up hope and to try their best to live their lives as if Aries were still with them. That is what he would want them all to do.

Lord Germaine asked that the Land of Taroc give them time to grieve, and together, they will rebuild the land again to what it once was. Everyone agreed. Archangel Michael returned to check on the family and to give them an update on Lucifer and Lilith. They will be charged for their crimes, and they will have to serve in the underworld for all of eternity. Lord Germaine and Lady Ashley both felt their son's death was avenged in spiritual court, but nothing can replace the loss of a child.

SERIES THREE

SOUL FAMILY SIX

Land of Taroc
Rise of Aries

SERIES THREE
SOUL FAMILY SIX
Rise of Aries

SUMMARY

Aries returns from the grave, but in reality, never was killed. He was purposely used as bait to draw out the enemy to protect the land his family built and the people in the land as their leader. He returns to his duties eventually, but the family he and his brothers created with their wives caused a brief hesitation.

Chapter 37
Aries Returns

Having mourned Aries' apparent loss before the entire realm, the family now strategized how to continue their lives with him alive yet believed dead. Their aim: to maintain peace by keeping his survival hidden from the world for as long as possible. Lady Ashley and Lord Germaine anticipated Lucifer and Lilith's heightened senses discovering Aries as bait. Thus, the Star and Hermit family devised a plan: to send duplicates of themselves to their children in the outskirts of the Land of Taroc, where they resided. Emperor Aries and Empress Sag received instructions to migrate further before the impending conflict, conveyed by a messenger owl. The creation of duplicate personas was crucial for deceiving the townsfolk and executing the plan.

While the Hermit and Star family remained in Taroc, their duplicates would manage affairs, led by Lady Ashley and Kayla, and Lord Germaine and Gary. Though physically distant, the duplicates would possess full awareness and sensory perception. It was unanimously agreed that their families were safer beyond the town's confines for the time being. With resolve, they departed to reunite with their kin. Aries and Sag, stationed a bit further away, welcomed Germaine and Ashley, sensing something amiss. Their arrival was timely, for they sensed the impending joy of grandparenthood, their instincts proving accurate once more.

Chapter 38
Aries and Sag's Triplet Girl Names

Ashley and Germaine were so excited to learn that Aries and Sag were going to have a baby, but Lady Ashley had a vision. She saw three girls. Not only was Sag pregnant, but she was pregnant with three girls. Sag passed out when she realized she was going to have three at once. It was easier knowing that she would be having one child, but three was altogether different. They weren't prepared for three, but they had time to plan. It was still very early in the game. The Hermit family and Star family were thrilled about having their family extended, and they took turns visiting their other children while visiting each other in between.

Empress Sag lost a lot of energy during her pregnancy, so Lady Ashley and Lady Kayla performed a few more duties than usual to keep the household in order. Lady Ashley and Lady Kayla prepared a meal for the entire family to have together, as it had been so long since they had all come together. Lady Kayla was very intuitive, especially when it came to her girls, and she noticed that they all looked a bit more sluggish than usual. She also noticed they had all been resting more. Lady Ashley mentioned to Lady Kayla, "Is it mating season? I believe they all may be expecting, and maybe even at the same time." Lady Kayla replied, "I believe you are correct," and she chuckled. They both did.

The entire family gathered around the table, and, for some reason, April, Venus, August, and June all exclaimed at the same time, "We are expecting!" The grandparents high-fived each other, hugged each of their children, and congratulated them all with warmth and excitement. That night was truly worth celebrating. For the first time, everything truly felt like it would go well.

But in the underworld, Lucifer and Lilith were coming up with a plan to get back at their former classmates for having victory over them twice. When they got their time from Spirit, they realized that Aries wasn't dead because they weren't serving time for his death. Instead, their punishment was to guard the underworld, and if any of them got loose from behind bars, their sentence would be even longer. They plotted to get someone else from the underworld to do their dirty work, so their former classmates wouldn't see it coming.

While all this was happening, Lady Ashley asked if she could have the honor of naming the girls. Sag and Aries loved the idea. She asked if she could name them Iyana, Meredith, and Tatiana Star. They absolutely loved the names and agreed to them for their girls. They all hugged with excitement.

Chapter 39
Uranus and Venus: Triplet Boys

The following morning, Lady Kayla was the first to notice that Venus seemed a bit larger than her other sisters, excluding Sag during their pregnancies. She promptly alerted Lady Ashley to take a look. Upon examination, they discovered three boys. While Venus was also expecting triplets, hers were all boys. The news sparked joyous celebrations among everyone except King Uranus. He initially passed it off, but eventually embraced his wife with joy once the news sank in. The family then began preparations and plans for the arrival of two more babies.

After the initial excitement settled, Lord Germaine started to sense an underlying unease about the safety of his family. Both he and Lady Ashley were keenly aware of Lucifer and Lilith's intimate knowledge of the law in the Sacred Land of Harts. Working within the system, they understood that the consequences for their crimes wouldn't involve the death of Aries, and eventually, they might still come after their family. In response, all the grandparents came together to cast a protective white spell over their future grandchildren. They chose not to burden their children with worries, especially during their pregnancies, knowing it could lead to additional stress or even premature birth. Venus, already showing more swelling than usual, was advised to minimize physical activity and rest as much as possible.

All the sisters were due near the same time, and each and every one of them was pregnant with more than one child. Every time they thought they had everything almost planned out, the plan changed. Lady Kayla and Lady Ashley made outfits for their grandchildren, and of course, all the girls helped, before the birth. No one knew the day or the hour that the babies would be born, so everyone was on high alert on what to do in case they all went into labor at the same time. Even though there was a plan in place, they all knew that things could change at any time. Lady Kayla asked if she could have the honor of naming her grandsons-to-be. Uranus and Venus both agreed that they would love that. She went with the names Kris, Kendall, and Kourtney Star. They absolutely loved those names for their boys, and they agreed. They embraced each other in a group hug.

Chapter 40
Pluto and June's Twin Names

Lord Germaine decided to spend the week with King Pluto and Queen June, lending a hand in preparing for their impending twins. Upon learning they were expecting a girl and a boy, and with his presence there, he requested the honor of naming them. Pluto and June, pleased with the idea, readily agreed. He settled on "Calvin Star" for the boy and "Lena Star" for the girl, to which they happily consented. This decision brought immense joy to Lord Germaine.

During his stay, he assisted in setting up a temporary nursery for the twins, as they were still outside the confines of the Land of Taroc. It would serve as their vacation home away from home. Once the babies arrived and were old enough, the plan was to resume full-time duties in Taroc. But for the present, safety dictated that their vacation home became their primary residence. The brothers, led by Lord Gary, collaborated to construct cribs for all the babies and adorned each room in every home, allowing the women to enjoy some much-needed rest and respite.

Lord Germaine realized that it would be better for the women to take on a different role in preparing for the arrival of the babies, with the men handling most of the physical work to keep stress levels down. All of the women happily agreed to this arrangement. They busied themselves crafting clothes and diapers in various sizes, as the exact measurements of the babies remained unknown. Every conceivable aspect of baby preparation was swiftly attended to.

While the Star and Hermit family planned diligently, Lucifer formulated his own strategy. He dispatched a spy from the underworld to observe the Land of Taroc and report back. This spy possessed the ability to transform into anything, making him exceedingly elusive. Known as "Hawkeye," he earned his nickname for his unparalleled vision and ability to move undetected. However, Hawkeye had a condition: he thirsted for more power. He demanded assurance from Lucifer that he could gain power, or at least siphon some from higher beings, in exchange for his service. Lucifer acquiesced.

Chapter 41
Taurus and April's Twin Names

Lord Gary made his way to check on King Taurus and Queen April, finding them visibly fatigued upon his arrival. Offering his assistance with whatever tasks they required, he was met with genuine appreciation for lending an extra pair of hands. Out in the backyard, alongside Taurus, Lord Gary set to work constructing a sturdy chest and dresser, while April took charge of preparing lunch and dinner. As they gathered on the back porch to rest, Taurus and April surprised Lord Gary by asking him to name their twins. Honored by the request, Lord Gary proposed the names Elisha and Eliott Star, which were warmly received by the couple. They shared a meal together, working well into the evening before finally sitting down to dine as a group, solidifying their bond even further.

As the family enjoyed their meal together in the outdoor area of the Land of Taroc, Hawkeye swooped in like a messenger bird. Lord Germaine, Gary, Lady Ashley, and Kayla all felt a foreboding presence in their land, but couldn't pinpoint its source. They anticipated something ominous lurking nearby, especially after Lucifer and Lilith discovered Aries was not dead, at least not to the entire land, despite what everyone believed. To throw off any potential spies, they never openly acknowledged Aries' survival. Hawkeye relayed to Lucifer that outwardly, it seemed like Aries was indeed deceased, judging by the town's mourning. However, he sensed the need for further investigation, cautioning that they were dealing with formidable higher beings who were likely aware of his presence.

Chapter 42
Leo and August's Twin Names

After a productive day of building and sewing, everyone decided to unwind with lunch at Leo and August's home. The day had seen significant progress, with work beginning on a mini hospital to ensure a safe environment for delivering babies. Lady Ashley took on the task of sourcing supplies from the outside land to support the deliveries, while also keeping an eye out for any suspicious activity.

In her report to Lord Germaine, Lord Gary, and Lady Kayla, Lady Ashley revealed that a spy from the dark forces had visited the Land of Taroc. She suspected that Lucifer and Lilith had dispatched them to ascertain the truth about Aries' demise, and warned that they might return soon. In preparation for any further intrusions, Lord Germaine pledged to conduct a thorough investigation to identify and thwart any attempts to disrupt the land.

Until then, it was agreed that everyone should remain at Leo and August's home for safety.

After everyone settled in for lunch, the family inquired if Leo and August had chosen names for their twins yet. They admitted they hadn't and asked for suggestions. After a flurry of ideas, Leo and August settled on Denise and Dennis Star for their twins, a decision met with unanimous approval. While the family celebrated the naming of Leo and August's twins, Lilith dispatched one of her spies, accompanied by Hawkeye, to gather information. Her spy, Hermon, was deeply loyal, a product of a past liaison who would go to great lengths for Lilith. Similar to Hawkeye, Hermon possessed the ability to shape-shift and track targets effortlessly. Together, they set out for the Land of Taroc to conduct further investigation. Meanwhile, Archangel Michael kept a vigilant eye on both Lucifer and Lilith, acutely aware of their abilities and their familial connection, suspecting they were plotting something.

Chapter 43
Delivering of the Babies

The time for the Hermit sisters to deliver their babies was drawing near. Lady Ashley found herself making frequent trips into town as the due dates approached, gathering necessities amidst minimal interference from the townsfolk or external forces. However, she couldn't shake the feeling of being followed or tracked. Taking matters into her own hands, she cloaked herself in invisibility and began tracing her pursuer.

Unbeknownst to Lady Ashley, the tracker turned out to be Hermon. Nevertheless, she summoned her messenger owl to discreetly monitor his activities and ascertain why he was tailing her. Though only sensing her essence as her physical body remained at home in the Land of Taroc, Lady Ashley remained on high alert, sensing something amiss.

Meanwhile, Archangel Michael was privy to the true whereabouts of the Hermit and Star family, excluding Lord Germaine, Lord Gary, Lady Ashley, and Lady Kayla, who were shielded outside the Land of Taroc within a forest field. He alone possessed the means of entry and exit, bearing both a message and a warning regarding what he had learned about Lucifer and Lilith, or rather, what he suspected was unfolding.

He spoke with the essence of Lord Germaine, conveying, "Lucifer and Lilith are serving their time in the underworld, but not for Aries' death. Their sentence is lengthy, yet they wield minions, or so I suspect, having seen two visitors meet them there." Hawkeye, capable of transforming into anything, and Hermon, Lilith's demon child from a prior failed assignment, were among their associates. Lilith had faced numerous assignments to the underworld due to her defiance and rebellious nature. Despite Archangel Michael's hope that their time in the underworld would reform them, that hope had faded.

He confessed to Lord Germaine that they were his younger siblings, and while he attempted to guide them, they had succumbed too deeply to darkness for his influence. Confronting them was as challenging for Archangel Michael as it was for their former classmates, given their shared gifts and familial bond. With that, Archangel Michael departed, assuring, "Everything I've disclosed is based on my suspicions and investigations to safeguard your family."

"Thank you, I will," Lord Germaine replied. The Star and Hermit families geared up for the delivery, gathering at the hospital they had collectively built and finished. Each family had their own room, with a grandparent accompanying them. Aries, Sag, Uranus, and Venus shared a spacious room with Lady Ashley and Lady Kayla. Meanwhile, Taurus, April, Pluto, June, Leo, and August shared another large room, with Lord Germaine and Lord Gary assisting with the deliveries.

It seemed as though all the Hermit sisters' water broke simultaneously, and they all began experiencing contractions. With so many babies on the way, it was clear they'd need extra hands for the deliveries. Lord Germaine called upon Archangel Michael for assistance, who arrived with Chloe. Together, they managed to deliver all the babies at once, turning the Star and Hermit grandparents from zero to twelve overnight. Though the delivery was lengthy, the joy it brought made every moment worthwhile. Now, the real challenge lay ahead: protecting, nurturing, and teaching the newborns everything they needed to become successful adults.

Chapter 44
Powerful Grandchildren

A week had passed since the birth of the grandchildren, prompting the grandparents to grant their children a well-deserved day of rest before diving into the responsibilities of parenthood. Lady Ashley and Lady Kayla each took charge of three girls. Lady Ashley quickly realized that one of the granddaughters was no ordinary child. She observed them effortlessly transporting themselves to different areas of the house, while another seemed to cause the ground to tremble, and yet another accidentally burned her. Recognizing that all three possessed unique abilities, Lady Ashley suspected that the others did too. Lady Kayla shared her observation, confirming that indeed, all the grandchildren displayed powers.

Understanding the importance of nurturing and guiding these abilities, they resolved to begin training them as soon as they were old enough. They pondered whether the protective white spell they had cast on their own children influenced the strength of their grandchildren's gifts at such a tender age. Some abilities remained unseen and unknown, but all the children, including the boys, possessed them.

Lord Germaine and Lord Gary rushed over as soon as they learned of the grandchildren's powers, especially after one of them accidentally burned Lord Gary while he was attempting to change their diapers.

Recognizing the daunting challenge ahead, they collectively agreed to delay training their children on their innate abilities until they reached the age of three. They understood the necessity of this decision, knowing that facing powerful adversaries would be even more arduous for young ones. Binding their powers until then was crucial to prevent accidental harm to themselves or their parents. Naturally, they sought permission from the children's parents, who wholeheartedly consented, understanding the importance of their offspring's gifts.

The grandchildren, though a handful both together and individually, displayed remarkable intelligence and an uncanny memory, traits that prompted Lady Ashley to initiate memory training from the moment they began to speak. Meanwhile, Lord Gary took on the task of teaching them meditation and the art of stillness. Referred to affectionately as "Grandma" and "Paw-Pops" by the grandchildren, and as "Granny" and "Grandpa" by Lady Kayla and Lord Germaine, respectively, the elders seemed untouched by the passage of time.

Over the years, the grandchildren absorbed knowledge from their grandparents and parents, primarily through organized group sessions of three. As each year passed, they accumulated wisdom, until eventually, at the age of three, their powers were restored to them. Thanks to the comprehensive teachings they received, they possessed the necessary control and understanding to wield their abilities effectively.

Lady Ashley decided to impart a white spell to the family, a concise yet potent invocation for moments of distress:

"Grandma, Granny, Grandpa, and Paw-Pops, Send your light swiftly, shield my soul, Envelop me in your spirit's embrace, Guide us from the unknown back to our home."

This spell would serve as a beacon of protection, a lifeline in dire situations. Meanwhile, as time passed in the Land of Taroc, Hermon and Hawkeye stumbled upon a startling revelation: the family posing as the Star family was an illusion. Their suspicions were confirmed when their attempt to ambush Pluto from behind resulted in his abrupt disappearance, as though he never existed. This discovery spurred them to seek out the real family. Years of surveillance and meticulous planning culminated in an attack that exposed the truth—they had been shadowing ghosts.

Chapter 45
All-Star Grandkids Disappear

The Star grandchildren had reached the age of five, fully embracing their powers. Despite their mastery, they hesitated to wield them unless absolutely necessary. Their reluctance troubled Lady Ashley, who often pondered whether they would rise to the occasion in times of genuine peril. Yet, she held onto faith that they'd act decisively when the moment demanded it, should it ever arise.

In the Land of Taroc, Hermon and Hawkeye meticulously monitored every move made by the Star family, keen to uncover their hiding place. They were acutely aware that they were dealing with elusive targets, akin to ghosts. To bolster their efforts, they enlisted the help of their demon allies, all coveting the extraordinary powers of this family.

Lady Ashley understood the risks of teleporting in and out of the land, knowing they were under constant surveillance. However, their dwindling supplies left her with no choice but to venture out swiftly, a task at which she excelled—except on this particular day.

Hawkeye observed both versions of her and followed one, while Hermon pursued the other. It all unfolded swiftly, but Hawkeye managed to track down the real family and began devising a plan. However, upon finding them, he was taken aback by how much the family had grown and expanded in the past five years. Tempted by greed, he entertained the notion of absorbing all their powers if they possessed any.

Returning with his findings, Hawkeye disclosed to his cohorts that the family was heavily guarded, with formidable protective measures in place. Gaining entry was no easy feat, especially considering Lady Ashley's remarkable speed and the invisible forest field barrier surrounding their home. This barrier posed a challenge, as it was imperceptible to the human eye.

Their strategy revolved around luring the children into a trap from which they couldn't escape or re-enter the protected zone. The aim was to abstract not only the essence of the children but also that of their parents and grandparents, thereby gaining full control—a bold ambition considering the formidable powers of the family. Nonetheless, it remained their objective. Resorting to typical tactics for capturing children's attention, they schemed to execute their plan.

They devised a clever plan, setting up a phony carnival adorned with toys and games just beyond the forest's edge, visible only to the children. Hawkeye lingered in the forest, observing the kids' activities, noting their preferences, numbers, and adult supervision. Before departing, he took the time to study them, knowing this information would serve as the perfect lure.

When the children spotted the carnival, their curiosity piqued, and they dashed towards the spectacle, entranced. Unbeknownst to anyone else, they were the sole family present, their existence concealed. Consequently, the parents remained preoccupied and unconcerned until they were summoned for lunch, only to find no response from their children, nor any trace of their whereabouts. Panic ensued among the parents, but the grandparents, recalling the teachings they imparted, hoped their progeny would rely on their skills and wisdom in times of need.

Determined to bolster their children's abilities, the grandparents augmented their powers, rendering them stronger and more resilient. They constructed a communal mode of transportation for traversing the forest, ensuring their return as a united force. Lady Ashley harbored suspicions regarding their disappearance and resolved to return to the Land of Taroc. Meanwhile, the parents would continue their search as Lady Kayla, Lord Germaine, and Lord Gary joined Lady Ashley remotely, employing their magical prowess from afar and maintaining telepathic contact with their missing children.

Chapter 46
Grandchildren meet Land of Taroc

The Star grandchildren were thoroughly enjoying themselves, but as the day wore on, they realized it was getting late and they couldn't see their way back home. They hadn't realized how far they'd wandered until everything around them suddenly vanished. Huddling closer together, they clasped hands, seeking comfort in each other's presence.

Hawkeye, Hermon, and their minions surrounded the bewildered grandchildren, corralling them into a box with holes reminiscent of a jail cell, and whisked them away to their hideout. Confined in the box, the children remembered Grandma Ashley's advice: if lost and wanting to return home, recite a special incantation. With determination, they chanted:

"Grandma, Granny, Grandpa, and Paw-pops, Send your light as quick as you can. Protect me with your soul and cover me with your spirit, As you deliver us from a place unknown to a place called home."

Magically, they vanished from the unfamiliar surroundings, reappearing in the familiar embrace of their home in the Land of Taroc, reunited with their grandparents. Overjoyed to see each other, Iyana couldn't help but ask, "Where is this place? It's not the home I remember. And where are our parents?"

Tatiana, taking in the beauty around them, replied with a smile, "It's beautiful here. I wouldn't mind this being my home."

Granny Kayla offered, "This is your true home. The place where you belong, not just a temporary refuge for uncertain times. You've returned to where you truly belong." Grandpa Germaine inquired about their journey and what led them to cast the spell to return home. Calvin explained how they had been taken captive, lured in by nefarious individuals. Lady Ashley proposed utilizing their essence, or a part of it, to trace back and potentially capture those who had lured them in the first place. Lady Kayla, Lord Germaine, and Lord Gary all concurred, deciding to safeguard the real children in the Land of Taroc with the essence of their parents, while the parents pursued the dark forces responsible for their children's disappearance, maintaining the illusion that the children were still with them. The grandparents then dispatched their essence back with a white spell, imbued with the abilities needed for defense if required.

Chapter 47
All Star Children and Grandchildren fight together against darkness

The Star grandchildren returned to what seemed like a jail-like box, their essence and full powers fully restored, as if they had never left. Before they departed, Lady Ashley affixed a tracking device to them, ensuring their parents could locate them if they kept moving. Lord Germaine communicated telepathically with Aries, informing him of their ability to track the grandchildren and providing directions to their whereabouts. Aries expressed his gratitude, to which Lord Germaine responded, "You're welcome, son. Love you, be safe, and protect our family." However, Lord Germaine didn't disclose to Aries that the children were already safe at home, wanting their plan to proceed flawlessly.

The parents followed discreetly, keen to approach without detection. The chariot carrying the grandchildren eventually halted, and they peered out at their unfamiliar surroundings, remarking, "We've never seen anything like this before."

Suddenly, darkness enveloped the surroundings, devoid of any visible life force. It mirrored the sinister aura lingering around them. Hawkeye approached cautiously, attempting to instill fear, unaware of the formidable powers they possessed. Although they refrained from unleashing their abilities fully, fearing harm to each other, those posing a threat risked grave consequences, even death, if they dared to attack. The parents keenly observed their children's composed demeanor, devoid of fear, prompting Aries to question if they were indeed his real children, though such thoughts were inconsequential; they were united in protecting them. Unbeknownst to them, their children harbored remarkable skills. In an instant, when Hermon reached for Kris, he was met with a blaze and freeze from Kris's fiery power. Witnessing Kris's strength, Hawkeye called for reinforcements, yet the grandchildren remained unfazed. Kris and Tatiana, wielding similar gifts, merged their powers like yin and yang, systematically neutralizing adversaries and ensnaring dark forces within their swords, which, despite their smaller size, boasted equal potency to adult-sized blades. Meredith and Kourtney utilized their wands to manipulate space, drawing the dark forces closer, facilitating their entrapment within the swords.

Kourtney and Iyana shared the gift of sight and teleportation, albeit with limitations based on their vision's reach. Their abilities promised to grow stronger over time. Meanwhile, Elisha, Eliott, Calvin, Lena, Dennis, and Denise wielded their elemental powers of earth, water, and fire against the encroaching dark forces, striving to contain them until they could be trapped within the swords. Yet, the enemies multiplied rapidly, overwhelming the grandchildren. In response, their parents rallied to their aid, joining the fray. Aries brandished his sword, capturing numerous adversaries, but their dwindling supplies became a concern.

Sag, wielding both her swords and her magical prowess, fought to ensnare the dark forces, while Uranus, wielding the Sword of Truth, faced off against a formidable opponent who threatened to strip away his family's gifts. Though Uranus prevailed, the enemy's words haunted him. Pluto, Venus, Leo, June, August, and April utilized their unique gifts to freeze, incinerate, and bury the dark forces, yet the adversaries continued to multiply unchecked.

Taurus erected a massive protective barrier, granting the family a moment to regroup and strategize. Amidst their deliberations, Lady Ashley and Lord Germaine arrived on black Stag, while Lady Kayla and Lord Gary teleported from the Land of Taroc. Clad in their armor and armed with extra provisions, the grandparents, though initially hoping to remain uninvolved, recognized the gravity of the situation. Engaging in battle was second nature to them, a stark contrast to their grandchildren's less frequent skirmishes.

Chapter 48
Grandparents join the fight

The grandparents joined the fray upon witnessing the relentless emergence of dark forces. While the essence of the grandparents remained in the Land of Taroc with their real grandchildren, the living grandparents stepped up to fight. They initiated the formation plan they had practiced, an emergency measure reluctantly prepared for. Taking their positions, the grandparents formed the front line, shaping their armored figures into a letter "V" and wielding bows with arrows poised to ignite and incinerate any potential threat. Behind them, the parents stood, their bows and swords forming a secondary "V" formation. The twelve grandchildren arranged themselves in a larger "V" behind their parents, covering the front, sides, middle, and rear, with Tatiana and Kris, the two strongest grandchildren possessing all four elemental powers, positioned at the back to safeguard everyone.

Once in formation, Lady Ashley dispelled the earth barrier created by Taurus and charged toward the dark forces, her gaze fixed on pinpointing the primary source of the conflict: Hermon and Hawkeye. Lord Germaine utilized his violet flame to transmute a significant portion of the negative energy in the air into positive energy.

Meanwhile, Hermon and Hawkeye returned to Lucifer and Lilith, withholding information for their own selfish motives but revealing the existence of powerful grandchildren. Realizing they were outmatched in this confrontation, the duo fled in search of additional assistance. Lucifer and Lilith, recognizing the futility of continuing to rely on them, decided to cut ties and pursue their own agenda, leveraging the newfound information to reshape their strategy for the future.

With this new revelation, the stakes soared for the family. Back on the battlefield, the transmutation drove many of the dark forces to scatter or become ensnared within the swords. Once captured, these entities faced spiritual imprisonment for their crimes. As the chaos subsided, the grandparents resolved to deal with the remaining dark forces, granting their family a moment to regroup. Yet, tranquility proved fleeting.

Hermon and Hawkeye seized the opportunity to challenge the family's authority, sensing their exhaustion. Lord Germaine, undeterred, charged at Hermon, confronting him with unyielding resolve. "I know your lineage, your origins," he declared, brandishing his shield to capture Hermon within his sword. He deemed it fitting for Hermon to face justice alongside his mother, rather than evading punishment.

Meanwhile, Lady Ashley pursued Hawkeye while her kin concluded the battle on the field. Each family member wielded their swords to capture the remaining dark forces. Hawkeye attempted to evade Lady Ashley by transforming into various forms, but her keen perception thwarted his every effort. Finally catching up to him, she delivered a decisive blow with her shield, rendering him unconscious. With Hawkeye subdued, Lady Ashley secured him within her sword before rejoining her family.

Gathering the swords containing the captured dark forces, the family summoned Archangel Michael to transport them to spiritual court. Expressing gratitude, Michael assured them of further updates and encouraged them to cherish their time together, free from immediate threats. With the swords in hand, Michael departed with his angelic companions, leaving the family to reflect on their triumph and savor their hard-earned peace.

Chapter 49
The Hermit and Star family have Victory

The Hermit and Star families had defected from Hermon and Hawkeye, along with the rest of the dark forces, but for how long? And was it truly over? These were the questions weighing on their minds. Though they had emerged victorious in this battle, they wondered when the war would finally come to an end. They had spent years hiding, away from the home they had painstakingly built, raising a family in secrecy.

Lord Germaine proposed stepping out of hiding, a suggestion met with agreement from Lady Ashley, Kayla, and Lord Gary. They knew their own strength and believed they could face anything together. Their unity on the battlefield had proven as much, effortlessly rallying as though they were seasoned warriors. Lady Ashley asserted their power, declaring they hadn't come into this world to cower in fear. They were a formidable nation, she said, and they must stand united, supporting each other without hesitation.

Lord Gary likened their hidden lives to the darkness that the dark forces had used against them, undermining the very land they had labored to build. Lady Kayla echoed his sentiments, relieved to discover they all shared the same desire to emerge from the shadows. Aries reflected on the deception they had woven, making the land believe he was dead, only to reveal his true survival. He wondered how their land would react to this revelation.

Sag offered a hopeful perspective, suggesting the land would forgive them and rejoice in Aries' continued life rather than mourn his supposed death.

The grandchildren buzzed with excitement about returning to their true home, the Land of Taroc. They found it breathtaking and brimming with activities and other children to befriend. Though they cherished each other, they yearned to experience interactions beyond their family circle. With eager haste, they readied themselves for their return.

As they packed and readied to depart, memories flooded their minds—beautiful moments shared, playful jokes exchanged in the cozy confines of each other's homes. Tears welled up as they gathered for a final walkthrough after loading their chariots in the grand house they affectionately called home. Lady Ashley, joining them, shed a few tears of her own. "Grandma," one of the grandchildren said, "we'll miss this home." In her tender reply, Lady Ashley reassured them, "We'll return for vacations. You needn't pack everything; leave a few things behind."

Excitement bubbled within them, though they felt a pang of finality, thinking they might never see this place again. Lady Kayla offered comfort, reminding them, "This is our home away from home. We'll visit occasionally when the need arises." With Lord Gary and Aries assisting, they loaded the remaining belongings before setting off. Lord Germaine and Lady Ashley led the way on Black Stag, journeying into the Land of Taroc.

Chapter 50
Returning to the Land of Taroc

Returning home to the Land of Taroc, Aries and the grandchildren slipped in quietly, unnoticed by the inhabitants. Their existence remained a secret within the land. Unloading and unpacking, Lord Gary and Lord Germaine soon called for a town meeting, inviting all who wished to attend to gather in the town hall for important news.

Lady Ashley took the floor first, eager to share the joyful news: she proudly announced her role as a grandparent to twelve children, a sentiment echoed by Lady Kayla, Lord Germaine, and Lord Gary. Lord Germaine extended an apology to the town for withholding this information and for deceiving them about Aries' demise. The revelation left the townsfolk shocked yet relieved at Aries' continued existence, though they couldn't help but wonder why it took five years for the truth to come to light.

Lord Gary explained their reasoning: they sought to protect the town and their loved ones from harm. By keeping Aries' survival a secret, they hoped to divert any threats away from their family. However, with the danger persisting despite their efforts to remain hidden, they realized they could no longer conceal the truth. Their duty to protect the town outweighed the need for secrecy, prompting their disclosure now.

Lady Ashley declared, "We are the founders and guardians of this land, and we refuse to be driven from it because of our inherent gifts. It's time we embrace our abilities and use them to serve and safeguard this land, as we were always meant to do." With resolve, she announced that Aries would resume his duties, as would the rest of the town.

The townsfolk erupted in joyous cheers, suggesting that the faces of Lord Germaine, Lord Gary, Lady Ashley, and Lady Kayla be immortalized as the protectors of the land. Unanimously supported, a ceremony was held to honor these chosen ones—the guardians, the protectors of the land.

The people of the town felt a renewed sense of security and happiness with their emperor's return. Anticipation buzzed for the unfolding of the next chapter, shared equally by both the townsfolk and their newly affirmed protectors.

SERIES FOUR
SOUL FAMILY SIX
Revenge on the Guardians

SERIES THREE
SOUL FAMILY SIX
Revenge on the Guardian

SUMMARY

Lucifer and Lilith learned of the family the Star family had hidden for years and targeted them and the Guardians for their powers to gain more power for themselves. They were driven by power in any way possible.

Chapter 51
Aries back to business

Aries had devoted so much time to protecting his family that he forgot about his duty to his land. Returning to work was easy, but feeling like he was neglecting his family made him guilty for being the emperor.

Before his supposed death, as Emperor, he had help from his parents and in-laws with some responsibilities. However, they've been called away more frequently as guardians to handle various tasks in the Land of Taroc. This situation has been tough for him and his family. The children miss them dearly and feel homesick for how things used to be.

He recalls how excited the girls were to leave home and socialize with others, but now they seem downcast, especially when he goes off to work. Aries' duties involve finalizing paperwork for town services like weapon production, water supply, firewood, and material procurement. Handling expenses for the large town and land is challenging, so Sag often assists him, which allows them to spend time together.

Although they appreciate this time together, both still feel guilty about not being with the girls more. Aries sometimes spends several days away, making it harder for Sag and the girls.

Initially, the girls were excited about the opportunities the town offered, but it's not what they expected. They spend more time training and attending school than before. Previously, they learned from their grandparents, which was more enjoyable. Now, they're less happy, prompting Aries and Sag to seek a solution.

Having the grandparents around would be ideal, but their work extends beyond the Land of Taroc, making it more challenging.

Chapter 52
Juggling work and home for Aries

Juggling work and home life was causing Aries anxiety, so he decided to discuss delegating some of his duties to the Kings and town citizens with his wife, Sag, and the town council. This would give him more time to be at home and work without leaving his family for extended periods. He realized that many of the responsibilities were a significant burden taken on by the guardians, their parents. Now, he understood the immense workload they managed behind the scenes, often with their families in mind. With his family at the forefront of his thoughts, he aimed to find a solution, much like his parents would.

Aries was en route to town in a chariot to review new plan designs and upgrades for the town, designed by Pluto and Uranus together. Suddenly, the charioteer stopped abruptly. Aries inquired why they had halted, wondering if they had arrived early. The charioteer froze, and as Aries stepped out, he noticed a wild animal on the trail—a lion, to be precise. Aries froze in fear, calling out desperately for his parents. Unprepared for a confrontation in his work attire, this unexpected encounter made him realize the importance of being ready for anything, as his parents would advise. He began to doubt his ability to handle his leadership role effectively, feeling overwhelmed by the unexpected.

Fortunately, Lord Gary was nearby on assignment and assured Aries that the lion was harmless, as they were together. Lord Gary ventured ahead to assess the situation before reaching Aries. Observing Aries's troubled expression, he inquired about his concerns. Aries confided that he didn't feel suited to lead such a vast land, feeling overwhelmed by his workload while his family suffered. Lord Gary reassured him, emphasizing his capabilities and the support he had from his team of siblings, in-laws, and townspeople. He reminded Aries that leadership takes time to master, with successes and challenges along the way. They pledged to return home soon to offer assistance, but Aries understood the importance of finding a solution before their return, as their assignments could take them away again unexpectedly. Aries agreed, continuing on his journey with newfound determination.

Chapter 53
Aries and Sag girls

Aries finally returned home from his business trip, eager to reunite with his wife, Sag, and their daughters, Iyana, Meredith, and Tatiana. They all rushed to hug him tightly, and he kissed each of them on the forehead, excited to hear about their day. They spoke all at once, and Aries replied patiently, assuring them he had plenty of time. They excitedly shared how they had been learning to transform and create things at school. Tatiana made a large fox creature that could speak and follow orders, Meredith turned into a messenger owl, and Iyana mastered invisibility. Impressed and inspired by their progress, Aries encouraged them to demonstrate. Each girl showcased her abilities, and Aries couldn't help but shed tears of joy, immensely proud of his daughters' accomplishments and happiness.

Sag also shared her creation with Aries, a tracking device designed with the help of her sister, Venus. They made it for the family's safety, especially for the children, knowing how easily they could wander off. Aries appreciated the device, reminiscent of the ones his mother had used for them. With Lady Ashley away in another dimension, the tracking device gave him peace of mind.

Concerned as darkness approached while the girls played outside, Aries decided to put the tracking devices on them. As they played, the girls thought of their grandmother and wished to share their newfound abilities with her. Unaware she was in another dimension, they decided to find her. Tatiana summoned a messenger owl for them to ride, knowing owls could traverse multiple dimensions. They found Lady Ashley in the midst of battle with dark forces, and she shielded them with her protective magic. After securing them safely, she ended her battle and welcomed her grandchildren into her protection.

When the battle ended, she asked, "What are you doing here?" and embraced them, saying, "I'm happy to see you all." They all replied, "We're happy to see you too."

Lady Ashley said to them, "Your powers are much more powerful than I ever expected for 5-year-olds. How did you know to reach me in another dimension? I know your mom and dad wouldn't allow you to come here on your own without them."

Tatiana replied, "I just asked the messenger owl to bring us to you, but we had no idea you were in another dimension and that it would be able to bring us here. We only wanted to show you what we learned in school, but we never guessed you would be so far from home and that we could do that on our own."

Meredith replied, "How cool."

Lady Ashley said, "We shall return to the Land of Taroc where you all will show me what you've learned. This place isn't safe, and you should be somewhere safe." They all returned home right before dark with Lady Ashley.

Sag and Aries were walking out as they pulled up to call the girls inside, but Lady Ashley said, "Not before they show me what they learned at school," as she hugged both Sag and Aries. Aries and Sag were just as happy as the girls when they saw Lady Ashley. Aries and Sag never even knew the girls left the front yard, let alone another dimension, so they didn't really get to test the tracker, but it's safe to say the girls can handle their own.

They all showed Lady Ashley what they learned, and she was as happy as Aries and very pleased to know of their capabilities. She then went on to say, "You will have to show me more later, and I am very proud of you girls." She hugged them all and said, "I must be on my way. I'll be back in a few days tops after I am done on my assignment." They said, "See you later, Ma," "See you later, Grandma," happily as she flew off on Black Stag.

Chapter 54
Lilith and Lucifer's plan

Lucifer and Lilith have spent the last few months devising a plan, with assistance from many in the underworld. What initially began as a simple scheme to haunt their former classmates for thwarting them in the Sacred Land of Harts has evolved into a deep-seated desire for revenge. Their quest for power led them to believe they were unbeatable, but they repeatedly failed to overcome their classmates. While they refuse to acknowledge their classmates' superior intellect, deep down, they know they were outsmarted at every turn. They underestimated them all, particularly Ariel, also known as Lady Ashley, now an Archangel like their older brother, and Lord Gary. Recently, they discovered that even Saint Germain, now known as Lord Germaine, has ascended to the status of Ascendant Master, making them even more formidable than before. Their plan is to attack their empire and everything they hold dear, including their beloved family.

Lucifer and Lilith stay abreast of their classmates' current status, despite residing in the underworld. They have allies among dark forces in every dimension and dispatch minions to destroy their enemies whenever they are on individual assignments. Recognizing their strength lies in unity, they know no one they send alone could defeat their classmates together. In truth, they likely couldn't defeat them individually either, which is why they send others first to assess their capabilities and weaknesses. They intentionally create distractions across dimensions to draw their classmates away from the Land of Taroc, where they plan to wreak havoc.

They are the protectors of the land, but currently, they are not present. Previously, there always needed to be at least one of them there, but because they set so many traps of darkness all over in every dimension, their assistance was required. It has been a slow plan of theirs, but they are now ready to start executing it. This plan has been kept secret for several years and months, and they are quite prepared to reveal it.

The original plan was a complete failure and involved Lilith's son Hermon, who later sought help from his mother and uncle after realizing he couldn't double-cross them without needing their assistance. Moreover, Lucifer and Lilith both felt it would fail, which is why they worked on their own plan for years and months. Lucifer and Lilith are still in spiritual jail but are due to serve as agents of the underworld soon to complete the remainder of their time. This will give them the opportunity to move about outside of jail and execute their plan.

They will be working for the spirit, as before, in the legal system, but they were demoted to the underworld and now seek revenge on everyone who caused them to serve time. Their assignment to the underworld as agents will soon be released as well, and when that happens, it's like unleashing the beast. This plan is very extensive and involves much more than before, and most are very tight-lipped about it. Whatever the true plan is, it can't be good for the Land of Taroc with Lucifer and Lilith involved.

Chapter 55
Guardians initiation

The day had finally arrived for the Guardians and protectors of the Land of Taroc to be initiated in the Sacred Land of Harts for their dedication and hard work and promotions recently received.

The first to arrive was Lord Germaine, known as Saint Germain in the Sacred Land of Harts. He was being promoted to an Ascendant Master, the highest level of prestige, for his creation of transmutation of negative energy from the violet flame into positive energy.

Second to arrive was Lord Gary, known as Gabriel in the Sacred Land of Harts. He had been promoted to an Archangel for his brilliance and intellect in healing and meditation techniques. Gabriel and Germain embraced each other as they entered the gates of home again.

The last two to arrive were Lady Ashley and Lady Kayla, known as Ariel and Angela in the Sacred Land of Harts. They embraced each other as they entered the gates and then embraced Gabriel and Germain. They all expressed how long it had been since they had been together like this and how good it was to see each other again.

Archangel Michael walked up to the four of them and asked them to follow him to the room where the ceremony would take place. It was at the Courthouse where Spirit held all ceremonies for those who had been promoted.

Since they all already had their wings given to them at different times, the last part of it involved the crowning. Since Archangel Michael was also an Ascendant Master, he crowned all of them with Priest Most High, and Spirit served as a witness.

It was official: they were natural-born leaders, ready to stand up for what was right and protect all lands, not just their own.

First chance Ariel got, she embraced Priest Most High. It had been so long since they had talked or seen each other that she held him, and he held her. The same with Spirit. They all congratulated the four for their hard and continuous service to the land and sent them on their way again for their last assignment for a while.

Before Ariel left, she went to check on Chloe, who worked in healing at the hospital. Chloe's eyes lit up when she saw Ariel. They cried and embraced each other for a long time, exchanging sentiments of joy at the reunion.

"I will come to visit you occasionally when I can," Ariel promised. "I wanted to see you before I left out on assignment again."

Chloe gave her some additional tools for her journey, and Ariel was on her way.

As she left the Sacred Land of Harts, she became Lady Ashley again, along with the other three guardians.

Chapter 56
Uranus and Venus boy triplets

Uranus and Venus's boys, Kris, Kendall, and Kourtney, are just as powerful as Aries's and Sag's girls. They miss their grandparents even more than they expected as well. They appear to be more miserable because both of their parents have taken more responsibility in the land. Even if they didn't get much attention from their parents, their grandparents were there to pick up the slack. They have been isolated ever since they moved from the outer part of the land.

The boys began to think about how they could get more attention. Kris thought that if they created something no one had ever seen or heard of, they would gain attention and recognition. Kendall and Kourtney agreed and went along with it. They did everything in secret and used all the scraps that no one else wanted to build a metal chariot that was child-sized. It took them a few days to finish because they gathered pieces.

They used metal to build the exterior, wood scraps from the town of Fire to construct a wheel that connects to the metal brakes to stop the chariot without needing a horse to pull it. They also added outside wheels to it, four of them, and attached used cups from the town of Cups for seating inside the chariot, with a strap made of cloth to keep them safely seated.

Finally done and ready to showcase it in the land, they first tested it to see if it would work as it should. Kris got behind the wheel and tested it. It worked perfectly.

They went inside their home, after leaving the shed, to get their parents. Kris asked his parents, "Can you both come outside to the shed? We have something we'd like you to see that we created." They happily agreed and followed them to the shed.

Uranus and Venus were pleasantly surprised that their children created something so fascinating at such a young age. It was innovative and something unheard of. The fact that they had thought of and built it to their size was even more amazing. Uranus wanted to see how it worked. He was thrilled and happy to see that his boys had created the best thing the town had ever seen and now wanted to have more made for the children and adults in town.

Uranus and Venus hugged their children and told them that they were extremely proud of their work. They wanted the entire town to know that they had created the next best thing.

He asked the boys to help him in creating more, and of course, they all agreed. It was just what they wanted to happen: more time with their parents, attention, and recognition.

Kendall said to his brother, "I wish our grandparents were here to see what we have done. They would be so proud, especially granny." It was fortunate that granny had returned from her assignment that day. They all wanted to show her, and they asked their parents if they could go.

Uranus replied, "She's on her way over now. You can show her when she arrives. She'll stop by Aries's and

Sag's home first, and then she will be right over." They all cheered.

Lady Kayla finally arrived, and she hugged each and every one of them. The boys couldn't wait to show granny what they created. She cried with joy when she saw it. She hugged them tightly and said she was very proud of their work. She suggested they could now work with their dad side by side to recreate the chariot in larger numbers for adults and children. It amazed her that both sets of triplets, girls and boys, had learned so much in her absence and at such an advanced level for their age.

In her mind, secretly, the girl triplets were a little more wild in their creations, and the boys were more practical in theirs, but that's what made them all unique and made them work so well together—their differences.

Aries loved what the boys built and allowed it to be used for everyday use instead of what's currently being used. He showed recognition to his nephews for a job well done. The boys were very happy and also got what they wanted, and now, comes more work, but they are fine with it as long as they share that time with their parents.

Chapter 57
Balancing work and home life for the Kings and Queens

Balancing work and home life for Kings Taurus, Leo, Pluto, and Uranus has been a job in itself with all the responsibilities of a King in town. Queens April, August, June, and Venus are finding it just as difficult to juggle work at home and work with spouses and then being home after school is released for the children.

They are all the same age and size, which makes it harder because they all have the same need: attention. They aren't by any means normal-aged 5-year-olds, but nevertheless, they still crave the attention of their parents and grandparents that they are all realizing they need and miss so much.

The Kings and Queens are also starting to realize how big of a role their parents played in the development of their children. They stepped in and did a lot when they were smaller, and now the Kings and Queens are realizing they could still use their parents' help.

The good thing about the children being away at school during the day is that they are excited about learning new skills and meeting new students and teachers. But not all the time will there be someone home right away to see what they learned like before when they lived on the outside of the land.

The grandparents worked more with them on their skills and techniques. They showed their parents, now hired help from town, accompanies them home from school and stays with them until their parents arrive. This arrival time is beginning to be later and later.

Kendall, Kourtney, and Kris usually go and work with their parents after school, since they've created another way to travel in and out of town. However, it's not only harder for the parents to be away from the children, but the children also feel a big void in their hearts from all the changes and don't know how to fix it.

In the meantime, things will remain as they are until Aries has a meeting with the town's council. He plans to begin allowing some of his duties and his siblings' duties to be passed on to a few other reliable council members. However, it has to be voted on and approved by the townsmen for all these changes to occur. This process may take longer than expected since all council members must vote, including his parents and in-laws.

Chapter 58
Grandchildren making adjustments

While the parents were brainstorming a plan to restore balance to their home and work life, the children decided they would visit their grandparents. But first, they wanted to create a way to stay in touch while they were away, realizing they might need help with this. They asked for permission to go after school with their cousins Kendall, Kourtney, and Kris to the workspace where they were working on a special project together. The hired help, Chloe, a former classmate of their grandparents who also happened to be an angel and their private guardian, allowed it under the condition that she accompanied them. The grandchildren were thrilled.

Deep down, Chloe knew the children were strong enough to handle themselves, but she kept a watchful eye on them in case they tried something crazy, which she suspected they might. She knew Uranus wouldn't let them interfere with his plans, but she magically intervened, allowing them this opportunity to create something big.

Tatiana, Meredith, Iyana, Elliot, Elisha, Calvin, Lena, Dennis, and Denise came up with an idea to stay in touch with their grandparents no matter how far away they were. Kendall, Kourtney, and Kris thought it was a great idea and knew how to make it happen. They used old metal parts for the outside and added their powers and tools to the inside to create a device that could receive signals to hear a person's voice on the outside. They tested one to see if it would work.

Tatiana wrote a spell to return to where she last saw her grandma in another dimension, knowing that if she could hear from there, they could hear from anywhere. The devices were made in sets so that both parties could hear each other without having to physically travel. Meredith thought it was a safer option than physically visiting, especially after their last near-miss. Iyana hoped it would work.

Tatiana arrived at the last spot she saw her grandma in another dimension, but as she arrived, a huge bird as big as she was flew towards her.

She said, "Can you hear me on the other end? A huge bird is coming towards me." They heard her loud and clear, and so did Chloe. She teleported to where she was and brought her back safely.

In that moment, they were grateful for Tatiana's return and even happier that what they created worked. But now, they were all curious about who Chloe really was. Tatiana asked Chloe, "Who are you?" She replied, "I am your guardian. I was sent to protect you in any way I can, but I would advise you next time to see what's on the other side of where you're going instead of going right into the fire." Tatiana replied, "Yes, ma'am."

They made many more with the scraps that were unused material and showed their parents what they had created. They all cried tears of joy, having teamed together to find a solution to one of the issues they were trying to figure out as parents and leaders. This was by far the most innovative idea this town had ever seen, and they had all done it together.

"We could use this means of communicating faster instead of relying on the knights all the time in the town. They could be used for longer pursuits since other towns may not have this yet, but we could create more to make it available for everyone with your help," the grandparents suggested.

The grandchildren replied, "As long as our grandparents have a set, we would be happy." Aries was thrilled that his children and nieces and nephews could put something together so quickly and as a group. He asked them to share more ideas for the town to improve its structure and provide a better balance between work and home. "You are more than welcome to come by any of our offices after school to brainstorm if you would like. It's welcomed."

The children were thrilled that their idea went over so well and that their input was welcomed. In that moment, with all that attention, they almost forgot why they created it, and now they needed a name for it. They called it the communicator – the perfect name for the perfect creation.

Chapter 59
Lady Ashley and lord Germaine goes undercover in the underworld

Lady Ashley and Lord Germaine began to see patterns in every dimension, as if distractions were purposely put out there to keep them away from their homes. They felt this way because the attacks were weak, as if the dark forces knew they couldn't be beaten and fled into thin air.

They decided to talk to Archangel Michael about going undercover into the underworld to find out what was really going on without arousing suspicion. Everyone in the underworld knows everyone else, so they needed to go in as animals to avoid detection. Lady Ashley chose to send a few of her messenger birds in first to see if they would go undetected before she and Lord Germaine committed to the plan. She even opted to send in fake birds in case they were destroyed and recognized.

They observed the messenger birds for 24 to 48 hours. When the birds went undetected, they decided to go undercover themselves for a few days to see if they could uncover any plans of attack or any other plans.

Before they embarked on this undercover assignment, Chloe brought something the grandchildren had created to keep in touch with them while they were away. She felt it would be safer to bring it along to keep the children safe from harm and from traveling so far. It was a communicator.

"I have one as well to keep in touch with you as you journey through the underworld," said Archangel Michael.

The grandparents were thrilled with the idea that their grandchildren had created such an innovative tool to use over great distances, especially considering their young age. They were truly proud as they began their assignment.

Lord Germaine took on the worst areas, while Lady Ashley explored a variety of locations. By chance, Lady Ashley stumbled upon information about a fake attack and numerous other false alarms across different dimensions. Alarmed by what she had heard, she quickly alerted her family and Lord Germaine.

Meanwhile, Lord Germaine learned of an imminent fake attack on the Queens in the Land of Taroc, designed to divert attention from a real threat. This news shocked him, and he swiftly disappeared to inform Archangel Michael in the Sacred Land of Harts and his wife, Lady Ashley.

Both were relieved they had embarked on this undercover assignment when they did, as it allowed them to provide timely warnings to their family. Archangel Michael assured them he would prepare additional troops in case assistance was needed.

Despite being in another dimension, Lady Ashley remained vigilant, her keen senses keeping her attuned to events in the Land of Taroc. For now, everything seemed fine, but she wondered how long it would last.

Chapter 60
Lady Ashley and lord Germaine message to Aries

Lady Ashley and Lord Germaine reached out to Aries on the communicator, quickly alerting him about what they had just heard. Even though the message was directed to Aries, everyone with their communicator on heard it loud and clear, including the children.

They warned Aries that great danger would soon flood the land and that it would be a while before they returned. However, Lord Gary and Lady Kayla would arrive soon, as they were finishing up their assignment. Lord Germaine and Lady Ashley still had some more digging to do before they could return.

They instructed Aries to prepare and alert the knights, pages, girls, and boys, training them for the unforeseen. Additionally, they told him to prepare the shelter outside the land for the very young and elderly who were too weak to fight, ensuring their safety. They emphasized starting with them because they were the slowest to move, especially the very young pages who had not yet begun training, except for the grandchildren who were extraordinarily gifted. Lord Germaine insisted that they be prepared only if Chloe was next to them at all times.

Aries and Lady Ashley agreed to these terms. The grandchildren, with their communicators on, cheered for the opportunity to stand next to their parents and grandparents again in this unforeseen moment. They all shouted to their grandparents at once: "We love you, Grandma and Grandpa. Be careful." In response, they replied, "We love you too. Stay safe."

Chapter 61
Lucifer and Lilith's plan partially revealed

Lord Germaine and Lady Ashley both returned to their previous assignment, hoping to uncover any revelations from the dark forces sent there as distractions. They waited for days, feeling like they were set up, as if the dark forces knew they were being watched and deliberately avoided showing up. Despite being in different dimensions, they shared the same sentiment.

Lord Germaine considered using his violet flame to lure out the dark entities, knowing it transmutes negative energy. The moment he ignited the flame, every hidden dark entity surfaced. They had been observing Lord Germaine all along. He managed to capture a few to extract information about the situation in the Land of Taroc. He sought to uncover who was behind the attacks, their whereabouts, and when and by whom the attacks would be carried out.

None of the captured entities were willing to divulge their sources, so Lord Germaine resorted to the Sword of Truth. One entity finally disclosed that the attacks were ongoing at that very moment, and the strongest force in the underworld would be responsible for the assault.

Lord Germaine released them and teleported them to the underworld. Quickly, he joined Lady Ashley in her current dimension. He flew in with his violet flame, causing every dark entity in the land to flee. He caught one, and Lady Ashley caught another. Together, they interrogated them, asking, "What do you all know about what's happening in the Land of Taroc?" Both had their truth swords out.

The dark entities revealed they didn't know much. They had been used as distractions, and whatever was happening would occur today. They admitted that not much information was shared with the distractions because everyone anticipated the use of the truth swords. If they didn't know much, they couldn't tell much.

Lord Germaine and Lady Ashley both thought to themselves that only Lucifer and Lilith would be smart enough to cover their tracks this well in the underworld. They teleported the dark forces back to the underworld and headed home on Black Stag, also known as Star, which is her birth name. The Star family got their last name from her.

Chapter 62
Lucifer and Lilith had all the Queens taken from the Land of Taroc

While Aries and all the Kings gathered all the trained pages and those ready to fight, the Queens gathered the elderly and the pages too young to fight. Together, they headed to safe houses outside the land to shield them from harm with the protective forest field. They packed into the four newly made chariots, which didn't require horses, and stocked up on essential items, preparing for a potentially lengthy stay.

Trips were made, but on their way back to the Land of Taroc, a sudden massive dust storm halted their progress. Iyana spotted the dust storm and teleported to the scene. There, she witnessed her mother and aunts being abducted by dark forces. Their eyes were covered, mouths taped shut, and hands tied to prevent them from casting spells or using magic. Iyana followed them, making herself invisible to avoid detection. She intended to seek help, but the dark forces moved erratically, making it difficult to determine their destination. She kept her communicator off until she found a quiet place away from everyone to use it.

She also had her tracker, created by her mom, but she turned it off briefly until she found a safe place. Both the tracker and communicator might attract dark forces. She needed a plan to rescue them. Wishing she had brought her cousins and siblings with her, she realized it might be too much for her alone. When she saw that gust of wind, she never imagined her mom and aunts would be taken. She knew she needed to think fast.

The dark forces surrounded the area and stopped at the furthest point of the Land of Taroc, where there was some seclusion, but with multiple dark forces. It seemed like they had been in the area for a while, making it their home. All the sisters, including Iyana's mom, Sag, were tied together on a pole, rendering them unable to use their powers or see. The dark forces were numerous, and their leader looked terrifying to Iyana.

He was a towering figure with a menacing voice and only one eye, but it seemed to miss nothing. His lone eye darted around his head, earning him the moniker Scar. Scar was infamous for leaving physical or emotional scars on those he encountered, making him one of the most dreaded figures in the underworld.

Iyana bided her time, waiting for the right moment to make her move. In the meantime, she sought out a nearby location to meditate and communicate with her siblings, cousins, and her father, Aries.

She discovered a secluded spot not too far away, though not too close either, ensuring she could keep tabs on any movement. An abandoned, tiny home served as her makeshift sanctuary. She kept it dimly lit and remained hidden to avoid detection.

Connecting through her communicator, she inquired if anyone was listening and requested they lower the volume while she activated her tracking system. No response came. Undeterred, she announced, "I'll keep my tracker on unless they start moving, just in case Dad wonders where I am."

Chapter 63
Lady Kayla and lord Gary return to protect Land of Taroc

Lady Kayla and Lord Gary finally returned to the Land of Taroc, just in time. Aries had reported that he hadn't seen any of the Queens since they led the elderly and young to safety outside the land.

"I haven't been able to find Iyana either, but I suspect she may be with them because her tracker and communicator are on, and she's very far from home to be alone," Aries added. "Unless Sag and the others decided to go further out for supplies and didn't say. I sense they are all in trouble. It's not like any of them to leave and be gone all day without saying they will be gone all day or without saying it to me. I checked on the outside of the land, and everyone there is safely put, but everyone else is missing that was listed. If Iyana and all the Queens are where I tracked Iyana, they may be in bigger trouble than I realized."

"The area is nothing but a danger zone," Aries continued. "It had been evacuated months ago due to some odd chemical that was never properly understood and is still being investigated and evaluated for the safety of our citizens. If they are there, we would have to go in with some health care supplies and masks in case the air supply is not well."

Lady Kayla and Lord Gary decided to finish investigating the leaked chemical so they could determine its toxicity and whether they needed to create a vaccine for their daughters and granddaughter if they were affected by it. They got to work quickly, but it took several days to finish. With each passing day, their concern for the safety of their family grew. However, they knew they wouldn't be any help to them if they arrived there and all fell ill.

Their findings revealed that the chemical could lead to hallucinations, sleepiness, dizziness, and even death over long periods of time.

Chapter 64
Lady Kayla and lord Gary the only grandparents

Lady Kayla and Lord Gary would be the only set of grandparents in the land for a while. Lady Ashley and Lord Germaine were on their way home, but it seemed they needed to stay in the field a little longer. Lady Kayla and Lord Gary had to locate the source of the problem in the Land of Taroc. However, to do this effectively, they needed extra help. Investigating alone wasn't an option, especially considering they were the only grandparents in town, and their mothers were missing and in trouble. Lord Gary suspected it might be a trap, designed to slowly harm them with chemicals if they resisted. He knew his daughters' strength and couldn't imagine them going down without a fight, unless something had incapacitated them. Lady Kayla shared his concern, knowing her daughters wouldn't stay away from family unless something was seriously wrong. Despite appearing strong for their in-laws and grandchildren, Lady Kayla and Lord Gary were deeply worried.

Realizing their children were in grave danger, they decided to call upon Archangel Michael, the Guardian of the Guardians, for help. They contacted him immediately through the communicator.

"Come in, Archangel Michael," Lord Gary said. "We need your assistance."

"I'm here, what's the matter?" Archangel Michael responded.

"Can you reach out to Lord Germaine and Lady Ashley and send them the supplies we've prepared for their protection and the protection of others?" Lord Gary requested. "We're providing masks and antidotes, as many as possible, for them to investigate an unknown chemical that's beginning to plague our land and possibly others. We need to investigate further to understand the extent of the problem."

Spirit intercepted the call, assuring them he would alert Lord Germaine and Lady Ashley immediately and personally deliver the supplies.

"Gather as much as you can. They'll need it," Spirit added.

"I've got Archangel Michael on this as well, along with the whole army. Many are falling ill with no known cause, likely due to this chemical," Spirit informed them.

Lady Kayla and Lord Gary sprang into action, fully aware of the gravity of the situation, especially now that Spirit was directly involved in answering their calls.

Chapter 65
Guardians called to assignment from Spirit

Lord Germaine and Lady Ashley received a message from the Spirit as they were heading back to the Land of Taroc. The message urged them to investigate a chemical being released in different areas of the land and possibly even in other dimensions. They learned from Lord Gary and Lady Kayla that this chemical was discovered months ago but its effects were unknown until now. Their mission: find out who is behind this and stop it before it spreads any further.

Before embarking on their assignment, they were instructed to stop in the Land of Taroc and receive further instructions from Lady Kayla and Lord Gary. The couple had tools and instruments to track the chemical, safety gear, and a vaccine in case they needed it for themselves or others.

Lord Germaine and Lady Ashley agreed and returned to the Land of Taroc immediately to gather supplies and see their family before departing again. Upon arrival, they sensed a frantic energy, but given the circumstances, they understood why. They greeted Lord Gary and Lady Kayla and assured them of their commitment to conduct a thorough investigation and bring the Queens back.

Though they knew something concerning the Queens was imminent, even their warnings couldn't prevent the events that were unfolding. However, they recognized that their efforts this time might not only benefit their own family but also the families of others.

Lady Kayla and Lord Gary provided them with all the necessary gear and extra supplies, including the vaccine, to use if needed during their mission. They reassured them that the vaccine was safe for humans and animals alike. "It's safe enough," Lady Kayla affirmed.

Lord Germaine and Lady Ashley received their vaccines and decided to check on the rest of the family before heading out on their next assignment. They went to see Aries, Taurus, Uranus, Pluto, and Leo to ensure they were all doing well. Understanding the worry that comes with not knowing about loved ones, they wanted to offer reassurance.

For the most part, their children were doing well, but Aries had a request. He asked his parents to check in with all the grandchildren and bring back their wives and daughter safely. Lady Ashley replied, "That's not something you need to ask, son. We're already on it." Lord Germaine and Lady Ashley embraced their children and wished them well as they set off to see their grandchildren.

The reunion with the grandchildren was filled with excitement and long hugs. Lady Ashley addressed them, saying, "We love each one of you. If you ever need to fight, give it everything you have. Don't hold back. You are all strong and work well together. Listen to Chloe; she will guide you."

"We're heading out now to distribute vaccines where needed, find the source of the illness-causing chemical, and bring back the Queens and Iyana safely," Lord Germaine added.

Before leaving, they embraced Chloe and urged her to protect the family. With Black Stag by their side, they made a stop where they knew Iyana was.

They all flew in, disguised as owls, to avoid detection. Finding Iyana, they gave her the vaccine. Luckily, she showed no signs of being affected by the chemical. Lord Germaine and Ashley hugged her in human form, administering the vaccine and providing extra gear for her and the Queens. They instructed Iyana to rescue the Queens and her mother without being seen. Lady Ashley told her to go invisible where the Queens were, whisper in their ears to let them know she was there, and give them the vaccine to strengthen them for the fight. Iyana informed her grandparents that her aunts and mom were blindfolded and roped together, needing something to loosen the ropes. They left her with all the necessary supplies, reminding her of her strength and abilities. Lady Ashley also gave her some fairy dust from Fairyworld as an honorary member, to use for creating illusions if needed. Confident in her skills, they explained they needed to find the source of the chemical spill and would have to leave immediately. They exchanged "I love you" and "be safe" as they parted ways.

Chapter 66
Aries has more responsibilities

The stress level for Aries skyrocketed when he realized that all the responsibilities fell on him regarding the entire land, the girls, and his workload.

He still needed to train and prepare all the pages for a battle that could happen at any moment, prepare meals for the girls, give them attention, and review all the orders and requests from other lands to purchase any services provided.

The Land of Taroc was known for their innovation, efficiency, and good work ethic, making other lands seek them out for service.

Chloe, guardian of the grandchildren, offered to help by keeping all of the children while all the Kings and Aries prepared the land for battle. She would cook for them, train with them, and asked Aries to relax a bit, ground himself, and stay focused on the land. "Try not to worry," she reassured him.

"Thank you, I am beginning to feel a lot better already not thinking about a lot all at once," Aries replied.

Aries began to gather all the female pages who were older to train them on formations and techniques. He made this decision because he knows what it's like to work with girls, having three the same age. He delegated King Taurus and King Leo to work with the boy pages who were older, King Pluto worked with the female knights, and King

Uranus worked with the male knights to prepare them for battle. The younger pages with advanced gifts trained with Chloe, including all the Star grandchildren.

Chapter 67
All the Kings have more responsibilities

All of the Kings' responsibilities increased just as much as Aries's. They all had work orders needing fulfillment in other towns, mostly requesting direct assistance from them. To maintain good relationships, they needed Aries's approval to appoint suitable replacements and to delay the work orders to prepare for a potential battle. They were stressed, as their wives and parents, who usually helped, were occupied elsewhere. They were stretched thin.

The Star brothers agreed to delegate these duties and assignments to the next best option. Aries signed off on it and sent a messenger owl to deliver the message. Communicators were dispatched to leaders in every land, informing them of the emergency in the Land of Taroc. Work orders would not be fulfilled immediately, and they were instructed to investigate a chemical leak or spill causing illness safely.

He asked that once they are able to resume regularly schedules worked assignments, for the next best men in town to handle those duties until further notice. He sent the messenger owls and awaited a response from each. He sent 8 owls with detailed instructions attached to the communicator so that the leaders in each land would know how to use it once it is received.

The leaders all received their communicators and responded to Aries' request. They all agreed with the terms and began to investigate in their land as well because there have been unknown illnesses spreading, but it has been slow and unnoticeable until Aries brought it up to other lands. They all agreed to help in any way if needed. Aries was grateful and replied, thank you.

Chapter 68
Female Pages training

As the female pages began their second day of training with Aries, he couldn't help but feel nostalgic. Working with them reminded him of his wife and children, causing his thoughts to wander and making it challenging to focus properly. In the town, everyone, including Aries, was consumed by concern over the Queens' disappearance and preparing for potential threats, neglecting to pay attention to their surroundings. Unbeknownst to them, dark forces were observing their every move, planning their attack based on the training they witnessed. They were growing stronger and identifying weaknesses, particularly among the inexperienced pages. Despite their temptation to strike while the pages were still inexperienced, other elements of their plan needed to be put in place first. Although the new pages lacked experience, their combat skills were formidable and would pose a challenge to overcome without the additional power the dark forces sought. Despite his distractions during practice, Aries considered the training for the girl pages a success. He commended them, advised them to rest, and promised to continue the training the next day.

Chapter 69
Male Pages training

The male pages began their training exercises with King Taurus and Leo. They worked tirelessly day and night to test their endurance, resting only after a full day of training. Lord Gary and Lady Kayla joined in, sharing techniques that the kings might not use. The pages were thrilled to learn from two of the town's esteemed guardians and eagerly absorbed the new knowledge.

Over the next two days, Lord Gary and Lady Kayla continued to work with the pages, giving the kings a well-deserved break. They engaged in friendly competition and drilled as if they were in real battle. These sessions proved invaluable, improving the pages' endurance, speed, and skills. They were immensely grateful for the opportunity to learn from such respected figures.

King Taurus and Leo expressed their gratitude for Lord Gary and Lady Kayla's assistance. Their presence not only benefited the pages but also allowed the kings to attend to other pressing matters in the land. It served as a reminder of the importance of their role in the kingdom.

Chapter 70
Training Pages into Knights

Training the knights was an even more difficult task for King Pluto, who worked with the female knights, and King Uranus, who worked with the male knights. This was because both male and female knights were either proficient in horse riding or skilled in mastering their weapons. However, excelling in both areas proved to be a challenge for many, except for those who had been knights for years. With a lot of new knights requiring additional training, King Pluto and King Uranus found themselves short on time due to other duties. Therefore, they sought assistance from Lord Gary and Lady Kayla whenever they could spare a moment.

Lord Gary and Lady Kayla, nearing the end of their assignment with the vaccine they had created, readily agreed to help. Additionally, they needed to instruct everyone on how to protect themselves in case the battle escalated into a chemical war. Each individual was provided with the vaccine and given protective gear, along with instructions on its proper usage during battle. The vaccine aimed to maintain their good health and shield them from illness or weakness during combat.

Lord Gary and Lady Kayla decided to extend their assistance beyond training the knights to include all the pages as well. They possessed techniques not commonly used by the Kings in battle, which they could pass on to the pages and knights. Both the pages and knights appreciated the unique and powerful techniques demonstrated by the

Guardians, making them more enthusiastic about their training exercises.

Chapter 71
Delegating Duties

A meeting is taking place in town to discuss the structuring of businesses across different lands and determining who will be responsible for future business affairs in each land. Those members of the town council who were unable to attend the meeting but needed to vote were available on the communicator to listen in and/or vote when necessary. All agreed to delegate additional responsibilities to others in the land to provide relief to leadership and prevent them from becoming overwhelmed. They unanimously decided that this change would take effect immediately.

After the meeting concluded, King Uranus began working on an instrument to detect harmful chemicals or other dangers for his family, as well as for his parents and in-laws. He opted to produce small instruments in bulk to supply neighboring lands and ensure everyone's safety during this unforeseen time. King Uranus enlisted the help of his sons to divert their focus from other matters, such as their mother's absence and extensive training sessions. He believed it would uplift their spirits to feel they were making a meaningful contribution, and he was proven right. They felt a sense of purpose in their efforts.

Aries, one of King Uranus's sons, suggested giving everyone a break from training to engage in various projects around town, allowing them to shift their focus away from combat preparations and towards enhancing the town's infrastructure.

Chapter 72
The Guardians meet with Archangel Michael

The Guardians had been pulled away on several different and difficult assignments together and separately in the last few months.

Archangel Michael decided to share with them how and maybe even why everything has happened the way it has. He shared with Lord Germaine part of the story of Lilith, but he feels he should share the full story with all of them about Lucifer and Lilith because there are things they never knew about their former classmates.

Since Lord Germaine and Ashley were still on assignment, they were contacted on the communicator.

He begins to tell them that Lucifer and Lilith are twins and that they are also his younger siblings. Spirit showed them grace after they had fallen from it in the Sacred Land of Harts during the battle against the land. He put them on a secret assignment to prove that they were willing to be obedient to the land without punishing them for their future crimes.

He decided to allow them a way back into his grace because they were really good angels and they were his siblings. They accepted his offer of being faithful citizens in place of not being punished for their crimes and took on the assignment.

Spirit created human form through Dan and Ava. Originally, it was only Dan, and Spirit decided to have a helpmate for Dan. This task was asked for Lilith. Lilith agreed to being his wife, but she wasn't going to be submissive because she felt she was above Dan. Spirit decided to create Ava instead as his wife and helpmate.

All they needed to do was obey the land, but because they were higher-level beings, they felt the assignment was beneath them.

Lucifer soon became attracted to Ava. He transformed into the snake he had become to persuade her to disobey and question the law of the land, leading humans into trouble like himself. He desired Dan's wife for himself and sought control over Ava. Convincing her to eat from the forbidden tree of life, he revealed its truth to her and persuaded her husband to do the same. When Spirit came to speak to them, he noticed their changed demeanor, as they realized their nakedness—a knowledge they wouldn't have had without consuming the fruit. Spirit knew the culprit but wasn't going to let this hiccup tarnish his creation. That's when the souls in the Sacred Land of Harts were called upon for a mission.

Lucifer and Lilith had no true intentions of obeying God, so he cursed them to work for the underworld, tasked with testing human weaknesses, a task they excelled at. Unaware for years that their former classmates shared this mission, Lucifer hoped Chloe would join but she remained behind as a watcher, guiding all of you. Upon discovering your human form, Lucifer and Lilith tested you at every turn, aiming to prove your similarity to them. However, they inadvertently revealed your strengths.

Even though the assignment was an epic fail, what added fuel to the fire was that Lilith became pregnant with Dan's baby, and it turned out to be a demon child. You fought him in your last battle in search for your grandchildren.

His name is Hermon, and he was following orders from his mother until he became selfish and greedy, craving power for himself. After returning the Sword of Truth to atone for his crimes in the underworld, he encountered his mother and suffered her wrath while in spiritual jail.

Archangel Michael goes on to share that he truly had high hopes for his siblings changing their lives and being on the right side of good, but those hopes vanished the day they decided to destroy the Land of Sacred Harts and everything thereafter.

The former classmates were shocked by the news of Archangel Michael being related to them in any way, and they felt bitter towards the ones who cared for them. It was a lot to take in, but the former classmates, now Guardians, can better govern their land and understand why things are happening the way they are now. They also comprehend why Archangel Michael left most of the fighting to them when it came to Lucifer and Lilith. No one really wants to fight their sibling or siblings.

Chapter 73
Lilith and Lucifer are released

Lucifer and Lilith have been released from their sentences in the underworld. Previously, they were in an in-between state until their sentences were completed. Now, they are no longer confined to the underworld, nor are they obligated to guard it by force. They are free to move anywhere they wish, as long as they refrain from causing chaos. However, deep down, Spirit knew that their good behavior would be short-lived.

They did what was necessary to attain their freedom, but Spirit always understood their true intentions. The moment they were liberated, they began working in secrecy with numerous souls from the underworld, many of whom sought revenge on the Guardians responsible for their incarceration. To divert the attention of the Guardians and prevent them from detecting any dark forces, Lucifer and Lilith orchestrated teams across different dimensions. They set traps extensively and concocted a potent chemical capable of inflicting mass casualties or injuries.

They wanted power, but they didn't want anyone to know they were behind the destruction. They weren't trying to go back to spiritual jail right away. They would meet for weeks until they had everything in place as they desired. They craved power, all power, and would go to great lengths to obtain it.

When Lucifer and Lilith were first released, though, they stayed quiet and low for a while to avoid suspicion, knowing they were being watched. They were aware their brother was monitoring their every move until he grew tired. They also knew that Archangel Michael would warn the Guardians of their release, giving them more reason to stay under the radar. However, even while keeping a low profile, they were plotting and putting together numerous plans for revenge.

Chapter 74
The Great Plan of Lucifer's and Lilith

Lucifer and Lilith had a plan: to overthrow the land of the Dragons and seize their power for their own selfish gain. Obsessed and driven by power, they aimed not only to steal the dragons' powers but also to claim everything associated with them. Competitive and egotistical, they believed no one could ever surpass them in anything. They yearned to regain their dominance, despite having committed unspeakable deeds against souls; they craved victory.

Their scheme was fueled by a desire for revenge against their former classmate who had bested them in a fight in the land of Sacred Hearts, leading to their banishment to the underworld for their crimes. This time, they planned to maintain a considerable distance in their battles with the Guardians, as they grew stronger with each passing day.

They are really impossible to beat. However, they believe their tricks could help them win against them and take them out, even though they cannot be killed, only severely bruised. They want them to all feel what they felt and experience it each time they win against them. They aren't revealing a lot of their plans to others who are helping them in this quest for power because they want everything to come as a surprise for the Guardians when they discover what's happening.

If they use their truth swords on anyone who knows their true intentions, the plan is over. They knew they would never be close enough in person themselves to allow the truth to come out. This was only part of the plan, but they have many up their sleeves.

Chapter 75
The Guardian's Findings

Lady Ashley and Lord Germaine embarked on an exhaustive investigation across every land, utilizing instruments crafted by King Uranus to detect traces of harmful chemicals. To cover more ground efficiently, they decided to split up for a few days. Their objective was to determine if they could uncover more than just traces of the chemical in question. Whenever they detected traces in towns, both Lord Germaine and Lady Ashley promptly alerted the local leaders and secured those areas. They diligently checked the animals and inhabitants living nearby, administering vaccines as necessary. Additionally, they left a supply of vaccines with the leaders to address any potential illnesses that might arise after their departure. Finally, after days of thorough exploration, Lord Germaine and Lady Ashley reunited somewhere in the middle of their journey, where they stumbled upon an abandoned building in the remote wilderness.

Chapter 76
The Guardian's Plan Executed

The plan to uncover the source of the chemical was put into action, yet questions lingered about why the Dragons' land was targeted and what lay behind the theft of power. The Guardians, along with Lord Germaine and Lady Ashley, resolved to return to the Dragons' land in search of answers. Before doing so, they decided to revisit the abandoned building where they had stumbled upon numerous encrypted messages, indicating significant activity. The sheer volume of messages suggested a well-established operation involving multiple parties beyond just Lucifer and Lilith, who were likely the masterminds behind it.

Lord Germaine opted to enlist a translator from the underworld to decode the messages. Using his truth sword, he teleported to the underworld to seek assistance. However, it seemed that either the inhabitants were unaware of how to decipher the encryption or they were bound by a spell preventing them from divulging the information. In a moment of inspiration, Lady Ashley conceived of a spell to enable them to read the words as if they were from the underworld, their last resort to ensure everyone's safety. Miraculously, the spell succeeded.

The disturbing truth revealed by the decrypted messages was a plan to plant chemical bombs simultaneously in every town, thereby annihilating entire lands. Although they had only uncovered a fraction of the bombs planted, the scope of the devastation was chillingly apparent.

They summoned all the Guardians, including Lady Kayla and Lord Gary, to converge in pairs upon each land. Alongside them came Archangel Michael's army, poised to swiftly thwart the unfolding malevolent schemes. Meanwhile, Lord Germaine and Lady Ashley journeyed back to the Land of Dragons, only to encounter a formidable challenge. Thousands of dark forces lay in wait at the gates, yet they managed to breach the barrier. Their companion, the baby dragon, darted inside to rally reinforcements, but the dark forces fiercely contested, unleashing their full might upon her. She bravely signaled the others, rallying those strong enough to engage, and together with the Guardians, they waged a fierce battle, vanquishing many adversaries along the way.

In the other lands, the Guardians executed their tasks with precision, dismantling the chemical bombs without harm. It became evident that the targets were carefully chosen, with other locations left unguarded. Lady Kayla surmised that the assailants assumed only two Guardians would stand in their way, underestimating their collective strength. "We're among the strongest field Guardians," Lord Gary affirmed. "Even so, let's lend our aid to our kin," Lady Kayla insisted. "Though they likely have the situation well in hand."

Reports from the other Guardians streamed in over the communicators, affirming their success in securing their designated areas, save for Lord Germaine and Lady Ashley.

With their tasks completed, the Guardians swiftly regrouped and set out to assist their comrades in need.

Chapter 77
Land of Dragons Fight

The land of Dragons was overwhelmed with dark forces from all corners. Just in time, the dragons arrived, their formidable power causing many of the adversaries to retreat. This created an opportunity for Lord Germaine, accompanied by the baby dragon, to ascend high into the sky and conjure the violet flame, a force dreaded by all who bore malevolence. As the flame engulfed the battlefield, transmuting the negative energy into positive, the dark forces found themselves vulnerable to its purifying might.

With the throw of the flame, the rest of the team swiftly emerged, fully clad in protective gear and armor, ready for the worst. Swords drawn, they absorbed what remained of the dark forces, their blades acting as conduits for the dissipating malevolence. However, the victory seemed fleeting, for Lord Germaine, Lady Ashley, Lady Kayla, and Lord Gary sensed the presence of Lucifer and Lilith lurking nearby.

Though Lady Ashley refrained from vocalizing her findings, she discerned from the encrypted message that the plan sought to shift blame onto others, masking Lucifer and Lilith's true responsibility for the orchestrated chaos. It was evident they aimed to seize the powers of angels and Archangels in their celestial forms. While Lady Ashley, Kayla, Lord Germaine, and Gary possessed the ability to fight in both human and angelic forms, those perpetually in angelic form were at heightened risk.

She shared her findings with the rest of the team and swiftly urged them to depart, recognizing the imminent danger they faced. Lady Ashley wasted no time in declaring, "We must return to the land of Taroc immediately. Our families are in peril, and we cannot afford to overlook the potential presence of hidden chemical bombs within our borders. Though we've only uncovered traces thus far, I suspect they are the root cause of this crisis. While we initially found no such bombs in our land, their absence may have been a deliberate ruse to divert our attention from the true threat." Lilith, standing closely behind Lady Ashley, remarked, "You're more astute than I gave you credit for. I underestimated you, but I won't make that mistake again."

In a swift motion, Lady Ashley seized Lilith and retorted, "I'm tired of your relentless pursuit of control and power," delivering a decisive blow to her face. Lilith, unfazed, questioned Ashley, "Why haven't you transformed into your angelic form to confront me?" Ashley's response was resolute, "Because you desire it, hoping to steal my powers. But I don't need my full strength to face you; you prefer to engage from a distance because you fear defeat."

Lilith's eyes widened as she realized that Ashley had indeed perused the notes. Without warning, Ashley struck her with a powerful blow, propelling her into the air. Swiftly, Ashley caught her mid-flight and tightened her grip around Lilith's neck, holding her aloft as they soared through the trees. The force of the assault rendered Lilith unconscious.

Upon reaching them, Lord Germaine inquired about Ashley's well-being and questioned the intensity of her confrontation with Lilith. He queried why she hadn't dispatched Lilith to the underworld with her sword, given her apparent invulnerability. Ashley's response was resolute: "That wasn't the true Lilith. I needed her to understand that I won't hold back this time, especially knowing she's watching." Ashley's intuition was correct; Lilith had indeed been observing, harboring a deep-seated fear of facing Ashley, knowing she would suffer greatly.

Meanwhile, Lucifer and Lilith were en route to the land of Taroc.

Chapter 78
Iyana saves the Queens and the Empress

Iyana absorbed her grandparents' instructions on rescuing her mom and aunts with utmost attention. Fearless and invisible, she slipped into the perilous domain guarded by dark forces. Stealthily, she advanced, ensuring not to alert the vigilant protectors. Finally, she reached her family, hidden yet unharmed.

Approaching cautiously, she inquired about their well-being. They affirmed silently, nodding in unison. With urgency, she relayed her grandparents' message, explaining the necessity of a vaccine to fortify them against the looming threat. Amidst the hazardous air, laden with a noxious chemical, she administered the vaccines, granting them fleeting strength and normal breathing for a scant ten minutes.

Delicately, she untied them, each knot yielding to her determined efforts. Prioritizing their defense, she armed them with masks and swords, anticipating potential confrontations on their escape route. The dark forces, consumed by their thirst for power, remained oblivious to the Queens and the Empress gaining freedom.

As they fled, the dark forces finally caught wind of their escape, launching a pursuit. Yet, fueled by newfound strength and armed with resolve, Iyana and her family braced themselves for the impending struggle.

They hurled fireballs, and amidst the chaos, Queens, Empress, and Iyana recalled the extra magic bestowed upon her by her grandmother. With a surge of power, she summoned a colossal messenger owl, capable of bearing them all, yet tragedy struck as her mother tumbled off mid-flight. Reacting swiftly, Iyana teleported to her mother's side and then back to the safety of the owl. Sag, grateful, pressed a kiss upon her cheek, expressing his gratitude, "Thank you, my darling, for saving us." Blushing, Iyana replied, "You're welcome, Mommy," before heading home.

Upon their arrival, they found themselves amidst Chloe and the rest of the family. Embraces were exchanged, tears of joy flowed freely; they were reunited at last. However, the reunion was short-lived as Lucifer and Lilith confronted Chloe directly. With determination in her eyes, Chloe urged everyone to stand back, declaring her readiness to protect them. Yet, Lucifer's chilling response shattered the moment, "They aren't the ones we are after, you are. You are the one who will need protection." Perplexed, Chloe questioned their motives, wondering if they sought healing or guidance. Unaware of the sinister plans brewing, she stood in her angelic form.

Lilith's retort dripped with disdain, "I'm surprised Lady Ashley didn't inform you. She always seems to outwit us, but it appears she's slipping." As Lady Ashley, Kayla, Lord Gary, and Germaine arrived on the scene riding Black Stag and accompanied by baby dragons, Ashley, witnessing Chloe's peril, swooped down in her armor, delivering a powerful blow that simultaneously struck Lucifer and Lilith.

After striking them, they vanished, yet Lady Ashley harbored the certainty that their full manifestation would never materialize. She confided in Chloe, detailing their scheme, and beseeched her to maintain her human guise to safeguard her powers temporarily. Naturally, Chloe acquiesced. Lord Germaine and Lady Ashley beamed with joy at Iyana's solo rescue of her mother and aunts, especially upon reuniting with their parents, Lord Gary and Lady Kayla. "Grandma, Grandpa," Iyana exclaimed, "I couldn't have done it without you," sealing her gratitude with a fist bump.

Meanwhile, Aries and the other Kings rushed over upon sensing unrest in the land. Reunited, they rejoiced in everyone's safety. Aries inquired if all were prepared for another skirmish. His intuition hinted at impending conflict near the borders of Taroc. With unanimous resolve, they affirmed their readiness, organizing themselves into battle formation.

Chapter 79
Lucifer and Lilith try to destroy Land of Taroc

Lucifer and Lilith had assumed they had ample time to seize Chloe's power, yet they quickly realized that the Guardians moved with astonishing speed, making them formidable adversaries. This newfound agility was the primary reason they were now prime targets. Aware that Lady Ashley had caught wind of their schemes, Lucifer and Lilith grappled with the mystery of her insight. They took precautions to exclude all denizens of the underworld from their plans and ensured that their encrypted communications remained accessible only to themselves. They understood the potential threat posed by truth swords wielded in interrogation, hence the need for utmost secrecy.

As they observed Lady Ashley's remarkable abilities, their own confidence waned, plagued by insecurities regarding their own prowess. This insecurity drove their relentless pursuit of Chloe's power, as well as the powers of other gifted individuals. Their reluctance to confront her directly in their true forms underscored their apprehension. Despite their doubts, they remained determined to harness Chloe's true potential, even if they lacked the intellect to fully comprehend it.

With their dark forces assembled and the ability to endlessly recreate their armies, Lucifer and Lilith poised themselves to unleash chaos upon the land and beyond.

They were all assembled and prepared to construct the chemical bomb, one capable of devastating entire nations with a single detonation. Previous bombs discovered and neutralized in distant lands paled in comparison to the destructive potential of this potent chemical. Those earlier bombs served merely as tests, determining the precise dosage needed to achieve their nefarious goals. Their initial plan to harness Chloe's power for added strength had failed spectacularly. Undeterred, they resolved to rely solely on their own malevolent abilities in their quest to obliterate the land in one fell swoop.

Tatiana joined Lady Ashley and Germaine, while Chris accompanied Lord Gary and Lady Kayla, each clad in their formidable armor. Taking up positions on the outer edges of the Land of Taroc, they formed a protective perimeter. Meanwhile, the remaining grandchildren, led by Chloe, and accompanied by the knights, positioned themselves at the forefront of the land, ready for battle. In the center stood the Kings and Queens, resplendent in their armor, prepared to defend their realm.

Aries and Sag swiftly outfitted the male and female pages, ensuring they were equipped for any eventuality. As dark forces encroached from every direction, the clash commenced. They fought fiercely, drawing their swords to banish the encroaching darkness to the underworld. Aries narrowly avoided a fireball, swiftly extinguished by Sag's intervention, while the pages systematically dispatched their adversaries, one by one, consigning them to oblivion.

Together, they fought valiantly, determined to emerge victorious against the forces of darkness.

As the guardians reached their designated post, they beheld the ominous sight of malevolent forces constructing something with potentially catastrophic consequences. Swiftly, they cloaked themselves in invisibility, edging closer to the unfolding peril with utmost stealth. They were acutely aware of the danger posed by the looming chemical threat.

Their strategy crystallized: permit the construction to proceed unhindered while surreptitiously pilfering the lethal substance from both ends of the land. Their aim was twofold: to safely dispose of the chemical where it could cause no harm and to substitute it with a counterfeit, deceiving the malevolent forces into believing they were on the brink of success. Chris and Tatiana executed this plan flawlessly, slipping in undetected to swap the real chemical for its harmless doppelgänger. Reuniting with their grandparents, they then traversed into another dimension to dispose of the hazardous substance discreetly.

Returning to the realm of Taroc astride Black Stag and accompanied by the baby dragon, the guardians and their grandchildren remained imperceptible, yet observant. The skirmishes below bore signs of prolonged struggle, with weariness etched upon every combatant's face. In a pivotal moment, Lord Germaine and the baby dragon summoned a colossal violet flame, unleashing it into the heavens. Its radiant brilliance vanquished the darkness, forcing the malevolent entities to retreat or meet their demise.

With the battle won, though Lucifer and Lilith still eluded capture, a wave of jubilation swept through the ranks. Their wrath was palpable upon discovering the truth: the catastrophic chemical they had anticipated was nothing more than a concoction of soap and water. Despite their retreat into hiding, Lord Germaine affirmed their perpetual vigilance, declaring their readiness for any future onslaught.

Amidst cheers and celebrations, Aries offered reassurance to all, declaring that indeed, all was well, and all ends well.

Chapter 80
Victory for the Land of Taroc

Despite the clear victory for the Land of Taroc, a heavy question lingered in each of their minds: When will this war finally cease? Even amidst triumph, the incessant conflict weighed heavily upon them. Lord Germaine offered reassurance to his family, urging them to hold on to their strength. He reminded them that there would be many battles they'd have to face unwillingly, but at least they possessed the skills and knowledge to confront them. He spoke of the need to rebuild their homeland, to elevate it to heights never before reached.

Aries nodded in agreement, yet beneath the surface, he couldn't shake his bewilderment. Why did their land require such extensive rebuilding? Why couldn't they simply live in peace, free from unprovoked attacks driven by nothing but lust for power? Lady Ashley, wise as ever, acknowledged the harsh realities of their world. She comforted her son, reminding him, "We may dwell in this world, but we are not defined by it, my son." With a warm embrace, he expressed his love and gratitude to his mother, thanking her for her unwavering support. In return, she simply replied, "You are welcome, my son."

Meanwhile, Spirit and Archangel Michael observed their Guardian team with immense pride. Recognizing the toll their tireless efforts had taken, they decided it was time for a well-deserved break. After months of relentless service for the greater good, they were officially granted a vacation to reconnect with their families, to revel in the joy of spending time with their grandchildren and children once more.

"Be the Guardians you are in your own land for a while," said Archangel Michael and Spirit. "We will be in contact soon." With farewells exchanged over their communicators, the Guardians embraced their family. Chloe, now officially considered family as the Guardian angel to all the grandchildren, joined in the embrace. Packing up their belongings, they collectively decided to retreat to their vacation home for some much-needed rest, grandchildren in tow. Racing to pack and eager to find solace, they finally arrived back at their home away from home. Together, they breathed a collective sigh of relief and whispered in unison, "Home sweet home."

Made in the USA
Las Vegas, NV
27 September 2025

28751474R00105